"Who do you want to kiss?" he asked.

Lyra closed her eyes.

She wanted his kiss, Dion's—the one person who had vowed to protect her like a big brother all her life. She wanted his familiar lips on hers—the same lips that had shared numerous fudge pops with her because they were their favorites.

"I—" She couldn't speak, couldn't tell him in words. Then again, she didn't need to. Dion and Lyra had always had a close relationship, from the moment she'd first set foot in the Donovan house. She'd related to him even more so than to his mother, who had brought her home. They were always in tune with each other. Now was no different.

Dion's hand snaked around her neck and tilted her head while he dipped his head closer—so close his breath grazed her lips.

"Do you want me to kiss you, Lyra?"

Her mind screamed no! But her body melded against his in defiance, her hands going to his biceps where her fingers dug in and held on tight. "Yes," she whispered, and then one of her many dreams about Dion came true.

As her eyes fluttered shut and fireworks exploded inside her head, Dion's lips touched hers with a soft sweep. Then both his hands were cupping her face, pulling her closer. She stood on tiptoe to reach him as his lips slanted over hers again.

Books by A.C. Arthur

Kimani Romance

Love Me Like No Other
A Cinderella Affair
Guarding His Body
Second Chance, Baby
Defying Desire
Full House Seduction
Summer Heat
Sing Your Pleasure
Touch of Fate
Winter Kisses
Desire a Donovan

ARTIST C. ARTHUR

was born and raised in Baltimore, Maryland, where she currently resides with her husband and three children. An active imagination and a love for reading encouraged her to begin writing in high school, and she hasn't stopped since.

Determined to bring a new edge to romance, she continues to develop intriguing plots, racy characters and fresh dialogue—thus keeping readers on their toes! Visit her website at www.acarthur.net.

DESIRE
A DONOVAN

A.C. ARTHUR

KIMANI™
ROMANCE

To the readers who continue to share
how much they love the Donovans.

KIMANI PRESS™

PLEASE RECYCLE
THIS PRODUCT IS RECYCLABLE

ISBN-13: 978-0-373-86262-7

Recycling programs
for this product may
not exist in your area.

DESIRE A DONOVAN

www.kimanipress.com

Printed in U.S.A.

Dear Reader,

It's time to introduce a new lineup of Donovans! Yes, there are more of those dark, dangerous and delicious men, and this time we're going to Miami to meet them.

Dion Donovan is definitely a lady's man, more out of habit than by choice. But there's one woman who's always had his heart. And now is the perfect time to tell her—except Lyra Anderson is engaged to someone else. Of course, a Donovan isn't about to let a minor glitch like that stop him. If ever you've believed in true love, Dion and Lyra are the couple to read about. Their love has spanned years of growing pains, relationships, heartbreaks and disappointments and is now struggling to be reborn.

I so enjoyed writing about this new branch of the Donovans and introducing you to another part of the family tree. This is such a strong and loyal family with scrumptious men and the strong women who love them. I hope you'll enjoy them as much as I do.

Happy reading,

A.C.

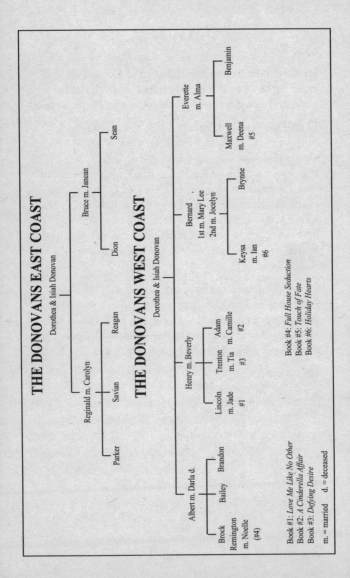

THE DONOVANS EAST COAST

Dorothea & Isiah Donovan

Reginald m. Carolyn

Bruce m. Janean

Parker

Savian

Reagan

Dion

Sean

THE DONOVANS WEST COAST

Dorothea & Isiah Donovan

Albert m. Darla d.

Henry m. Beverly

Bernard
1st m. Mary Lee
2nd m. Jocelyn

Everette
m. Alma

Brock

Bailey

Brandon

Lincoln
m. Jade
#1

Trenton
m. Tia
#3

Adam
m. Camille
#2

Keysa
m. Ian
#6

Brynne

Maxwell
m. Deena
#5

Benjamin

Remington
m. Noelle
(#4)

Book #1: *Love Me Like No Other*
Book #2: *A Cinderella Affair*
Book #3: *Defying Desire*

Book #4: *Full House Seduction*
Book #5: *Touch of Fate*
Book #6: *Holiday Hearts*

m. = married   d. = deceased

Prologue

Miami: ten years ago…

"Give me a reason why I should stay, Dion." She looked into his eyes, which reflected a serious, intense gaze that furrowed his brow slightly.

Lyra knew that look well, had stared into those eyes more times then she could count. But today was different. She was different, and their circumstances were undeniably different. What had transpired between them after the prom a month ago had changed everything. It had been an ordinary Saturday night—indigo sky, no stars and a warm summer-night breeze. She was talking to her best friend in the entire world after one of the worst nights of her life.

But just like the shifting tides along the stretch of beach behind what locals called the Donovan Big House,

Lyra's and Dion's lives would forever be changed from that moment on. If Lyra were inclined toward clichés, she would say that now was her moment of truth. Since she prided herself on being a realist, she decided it was her day of reckoning instead. Dion Donovan did not love her. At least not in the way she desperately wanted him to. And that, for Lyra, was a huge problem.

"You should do what's best for you, Lyra. I've always told you that," he'd said.

She sighed, gave a little chuckle because his words weren't totally unexpected.

"Is that your way of telling me to go?" she'd said.

The clench of his jaw was the only telltale sign that this wasn't as easy for him as Lyra thought.

"I'm telling you that it's time you start thinking of yourself, taking care of you and what's important to you. Photography is important, it's all you've been doing and talking about since I've known you," he'd said.

There was a breeze that morning as they stood on the balcony of the mansion, where Lyra had enjoyed growing up the past ten years. It was a sprawling estate in south Miami that boasted all the luxury and opulence of this branch of the Donovan family tree, who were making their mark in the entertainment industry. Although they were close, the West Coast Donovans were into oil and casinos.

"I can study photography anywhere" was Lyra's response. She grimaced inside at the thought of how needy it sounded.

"I want you to have the best, you know that. The best schools…." He cleared his throat. "The best life."

Lifting her head she met his gaze once more. She looked him in the eye, and yet he was brushing her feelings away. Her heart would break but she would survive, because she didn't know how to do anything else.

"Then tell me to go."

He extended his arm as her heart hammered in her chest. Dion gently traced his fingertips along her jawline, hesitating slightly as he approached her lips. Of course her lips parted. She wanted his kiss again, had wanted it with a desperate hunger since that night. But he wouldn't give it to her. She knew that as well as she knew that in an hour she'd be on a plane to Los Angeles—alone.

"Go," he said finally. "Go and be happy."

Lyra had no idea whether it was fury or the onrushing pangs of hurt that overwhelmed her, but she gave him a curt nod and turned her back to him and rushed back into the house. All she knew was that she was going to take his advice. She was going to leave Miami and make a life for herself—on her own terms—and be happy. Without the man she loved.

Chapter 1

Family dinners at the Big House were usually entertaining. Tonight, however, Dion Donovan knew this one would be even more so. He knew the announcement that his mother, Janean, was going to make would be delivered with all the formality and fanfare she possessed. He hadn't liked it when he'd heard the news earlier in the week and he disliked it even more now.

Entering through the large white double doors, Dion inhaled deeply and immediately felt at home. It made perfect sense, considering he'd grown up in the lavish Key Biscayne estate with his family.

Dinner at his parents' house was a monthly affair, a usually uneventful evening with his younger brother and sister that kept his parents, Janean and Bruce Donovan, from focusing on the fact that he was still happily single. This afternoon would be different. It wasn't just a normal family dinner. All the Miami Donovans were invited, including his uncle Reginald and aunt Carolyn and their three children. It always took place once a month on a Sunday afternoon, after everyone had returned from church. There was plenty of food and laughter and just plain family fun. Any other Sunday afternoon, Dion might have looked forward to the gathering. Today, he simply hoped the familial conversation would hide what was truly on his mind.

"Hey, man, expected to see you earlier," said Sean Donovan. Dion's younger brother by three years greeted him in the foyer, no doubt having been booted out of the kitchen by their mother for sneaking a taste of the food.

Dion shook his brother's hand. "I had a few things to go over for tomorrow's meeting," he said. "I'll be tied up in the morning, so I wanted to make sure I had time to review everything I want to discuss."

Sean nodded. "We're meeting at one o'clock in your office, correct?"

"Correct."

Dion was the editor in chief of *Infinity Magazine,* a quickly growing publication that focused on up-and-coming African-American businesses, entertainers and the movers and shakers in the black community. Bruce Donovan, along with his brother Reginald owned the DNT Network, a cable television company, which in addition to launching *Infinity Magazine* also owned Donovan Management Company, a literary, sports and talent agency that handled more than a hundred clients.

The Donovans in Las Vegas—Everette and Henry—were in the oil business and had also founded an international charity. Thus far, Dion Donovan's family in Miami had focused their efforts on the media and entertainment fields, and it was proving to be quite profitable.

Sean was one of the managing editors at *Infinity* and reported directly to Dion. They'd experienced the usual sibling rivalry growing up, and Sean and Dion's working relationship was often as intense as their family dynamic. Still, they kept their eyes on the prize—*Infinity* was in their blood and no matter what their disagreements were they always managed to pull together to make the best decisions for the magazine and the family.

"I've been working on that new distribution deal, so we should discuss that," Sean said as both men walked toward the living room.

The living room was one of the largest spaces on the first floor of the house. Although it was a place for family gatherings that was furnished in a modern European style—with beige, deep-cushioned Italian leather sofas, lush dark-brown rugs, light oak coffee and end tables and a massive bar along the far wall—it still had a comfortable feel. The space was dubbed the centerpiece of the Big House by the Donovan children when they were young. The fact that the house was situated directly on the water with its own private dock and a breathtaking view made them think they were some kind of royalty— black royalty, as Janean would often say.

"Good." Dion nodded. "That's exactly what I want to talk about, moving the magazine forward for all of us."

Dion fixed himself a drink as he talked.

Sean took a seat on the recliner. "You okay?" he asked.

"What kind of question is that?" Dion responded with a frown. "Of course I'm okay."

Sean observed his brother in the calm, careful way

he always had. "Then why are you fixing yourself a glass of rum? You hate rum."

Dion looked down at his glass and was about to say something, but put the glass down instead. "Preoccupied, I guess."

With a knowing nod Sean kept staring, a look that Dion knew meant he didn't believe a word he'd just said. It was that way with him and Sean. The three-year age difference didn't really matter; sometimes they seemed as close as twins. He could complete Sean's sentences and pick up on his moods, just as Sean could read him. The two Donovan boys were known for their good looks and wealth. They were also smart, both having graduated from Columbia, their father's alma mater. Janean loved and spoiled her boys as much as Bruce would let her, but she'd always wanted a daughter. The day she brought home Lyra Anderson, she found just what she'd been looking for.

Sean and Dion weren't thrilled about having a sister, but over the years they had grown to love her like a sister and keep a protective eye on her. They treated her just like she was related by blood, and in return she treated them and their parents like family.

Still, the fact remained that Lyra *wasn't* their sister. And that, Dion had realized years ago, was a big problem.

"I'm cool," he said trying to assure Sean. When his father walked in, Dion welcomed the distraction. "Hey, Dad," he said, turning away from Sean toward his father.

"Dion! Sean!" the elder Donovan said in his booming voice as he made a beeline straight for the sofa. "Your mother has had me working all day, like some kind of hired help." He rubbed his hand down the back of his neck and plopped down like he'd been dying to sit and relax all day.

Bruce Donovan was a tall, broad man, who had just a sprinkling of gray hair peppering his otherwise short dark brown curls. The gray gave him a distinguished look that only added to the impeccable reputation that Bruce was known for. More often than not he wore dress pants and a dress shirt—with or without a tie, depending on his schedule for the day—but he had a laid-back attitude that often disarmed his colleagues and made them think he was a pushover, which he definitely was not.

"You know how she is when it's the family dinner night," Sean said, chuckling.

Bruce shook his head. "I don't know why. It's just the family. Everybody knows what the house looks like on good and bad days. You'd think she was entertaining the king and queen or some other foolishness."

"Why doesn't she hire a maid?" Dion asked—a question he already knew the answer to. Still, it bothered him that his mother, at sixty-one, was working like a woman half her age.

"Now you know that's not going to happen," Sean replied.

"And don't you let her hear you asking about it, either," Bruce chimed in with a warning glare that belied his amusement. "She'll bust your butt for even uttering the idea that she needs help with this house."

Dion laughed along with his father and his brother, enjoying the family joke. It had always been that way with his family. They could laugh and cry together and talk about anything. Bruce and Janean had long ago taught them to be open and honest in the Donovan household. The thought made Dion's stomach knot with regret. He hadn't been honest with himself years ago, and because of that he'd ruined what might have been the best friendship he'd ever had. Now she was coming home, and Dion didn't know how he was going to handle that.

Lyra was going home.

She'd stepped off the plane at Miami International, taking a commercial flight rather than the private jet the Donovans had offered. When she'd left ten years ago, it had been on that private jet, taking her across the country to begin her new life. Now she was back, and everything was different. She had no idea if that was going to be a good or bad thing.

Knocking on the door felt strange, but Lyra lifted the heavy brass knocker and let it clang against the door. All the while she took deep steadying breaths, drawing upon everything she'd learned in yoga class about centering herself and clearing her mind. When the door swung open, all that centering and mind-clearing fled as she was quickly scooped up into strong arms and spun around so that her feet didn't even touch the floor.

"Little Lyra! You're back!" Parker Donovan said in his smooth as silk voice that was lined with the barest hint of humor. Parker was Reginald and Carolyn Donovan's oldest son, Dion and Sean's first cousin, and one of the many big brother figures Lyra had while growing up.

"Hi, Parker. You can put me down now. I'm not Little Lyra anymore," she said, unable to contain her laughter as he set her petite five-foot-five, one-hundred-and-twenty-pound frame down on the floor again.

"You still look little to me," he said, continuing to smile at her and giving her a soft punch on the shoulder. "Just a bit more tanned, but still little and pretty as ever."

Lyra smiled up at him, remembering his cool gray-green eyes and dark skin tone. Several of the Donovan men had the same eyes, which only added to their attractiveness. From a distance she could hear the laughter and chatter of the other Donovan family members. Sunday dinners for the Donovans were a must to attend, and the only acceptable excuse was death or being as close to death as one could possibly be.

"Gang's all here, huh?" she said, knowing she was stalling.

"You know how these dinners go," he said with a shrug.

And she did know, Lyra thought as she looked around. The décor had changed a bit, much more modern than it had been when she'd left, but still warm and welcoming. She glanced around the foyer, across the shining champagne-and-gold marbled floor, up the winding staircase with its thick banister and wide stairs. Her room used to be all the way down the hall to the left. She had a huge canopy bed, a window with a small balcony, plush carpet, lovely draperies, a desk, a closet full of clothes and practically everything a girl could ever want—even if she wasn't a member of the Donovan family, biologically speaking.

"And the prodigal daughter returns."

Lyra heard his voice and felt warmth spiral through her spine, sliding downward like a warm waterfall. She needed another moment, another couple of minutes or an hour to gather herself before seeing him. Unfortunately, it didn't look like she was going to get it.

"She's all grown up now, man. Doesn't she look good?" Parker asked, and Lyra wanted to kick him as she had so many times in the past. He always did have a knack for saying what others wanted kept quiet. His playfulness was a big part of his adorable personality, but right now was a pain in her behind. She slowly turned, having decided it was time to face the inevitable.

"Hey, Dion," she said with all the casual aloofness she could muster.

He walked toward her. He still had the tall muscular body she remembered as if it were yesterday. He didn't smile. His look was much more intense. Dion Donovan stood at least six feet six inches tall, with a honey complexion, short-cropped black hair and a swagger that said he looked good even if you didn't want to admit it. He wore jeans and a T-shirt that hugged every inch of his eight-pack and wrapped around his thick biceps like candy coating.

"Hey, Lyra. It's good to see you," he said as he came closer.

He was going to hug her, Lyra knew. Not as eagerly as Parker had, but he would wrap his arms around her, because that's how the Donovans were with family. And she was family, she reminded herself. She'd grown up in this house, had been taken in because her own mother couldn't seem to get her act together. Janean and Bruce Donovan had raised her as one of their own, giving her every advantage and expecting just as much from her as they did their own children. She owed them everything.

She especially owed them the respect of not pining after their eldest son as if he were the only man on earth that could make her body hum with arousal. Even though, the fact still remained, he was.

"It's good to see you, too," she managed as soon as his hands brushed her shoulders and he pulled her up close. He smelled wonderful—some expensive and insanely sexy cologne that she knew would stay with her for days to come.

"I missed you," he whispered in her ear and Lyra remained silent.

She wouldn't say the same, couldn't tell him how much she'd missed him. It was pointless, and she'd made a promise not to move backward. Her new life was her future. Reviving feelings from the past was a futile and emotionally self-destructive exercise, and that was something she refused to engage in. But she'd missed the hell out of him, too.

Chapter 2

Food was everywhere, on fine china platters and
crystal and silver condiment bowls and trays along
the length of the eight-foot mahogany table covered in
an antique-lace tablecloth. Candied yams, homemade
macaroni and cheese, corn bread, a huge baked turkey,
glazed pineapple ham, mashed potatoes, corn bread
stuffing, green beans and corn was more than Lyra
could take in in one glance. The dining room hadn't
changed much since she'd left. The massive table was
still in the center of the room with chairs all around it,
the large china cabinet that spread across the expanse
of champagne-colored walls was filled with expensive
china patterns, even though several of the pieces were
being used on the table and the sideboard, which held
even more food.

The atmosphere felt homely, warm and welcoming,

and the people sitting and standing around the table greeted her in a way that echoed those feelings.

"You're back!" Regan Donovan was across the room in seconds, her long arms wrapping around Lyra before she could do anything but smile.

Lyra stumbled back a step as Regan embraced her. "Hey, Regan. It's good to see you, too."

"Oh, my God! When I got your email I was ecstatic. You know we need to get together so we can catch up. We can't do that here with everybody around, but I want to hear everything that's happened in L.A. And I mean *everything*," she said, her large expressive eyes indicating that she wanted to hear things Lyra couldn't talk about around the rest of the Donovans.

"Let her go, Regan. The rest of us would like to say hello, too." Savian, Regan Donovan's older brother, pushed her aside.

"Hi, Savian," Lyra said, welcoming a hug from the quiet and reserved Donovan cousin, who rarely ever smiled. But there was still a warmth and sincerity evident in his hazel eyes.

"Hey, kiddo. I see you survived it out there in la-la land."

"I did." She smiled, pulling away from him. "It wasn't so bad," she said biting her inner cheek to keep from blurting out how bad those years away had really been. It wasn't anybody's business she'd told herself. She'd left to pursue her goals to become a photographer. And in that regard, she'd done pretty damned well for herself. It was everything else that had fallen apart.

"Well, you look fabulous," said Carolyn Donovan, a tall, slim woman with a warm chocolate complexion and hair that had a silvery glow. She was beautiful and looked elegant in her cream-colored linen slacks and pale pink blouse. Her hair was flawless as usual and just barely grazed her shoulders. Her eyes smiled as she reached out to hug Lyra.

"Aunt Carolyn, it's good to see you."

"Yes," Carolyn said when she released Lyra from her grip, putting her hands on Lyra's shoulders as she continued looking her up and down. "Just fabulous. The sun's kissed your skin so you look even more Native American then you did when you were a little girl. And you've blossomed."

Lyra didn't know she could still blush, but the heat in her cheeks said she hadn't grown out of that habit. The Donovans had always told her of her Native American heritage, to which Lyra simply smiled and nodded. She'd never known her father, and her mother, Paula Anderson, certainly wasn't Native American. She was an African-American, and had grown up in the Lemon City area of Miami, which was known for its large community of Haitian immigrants. But that's where Mama Nell, Lyra's grandmother, had lived, so that's where Paula grew up until she felt like she was old enough to make it on her own. But Lyra's mother thought she was grown the minute she learned to talk, and at age thirteen Paula took to the streets because Mama Nell's restrictions were too strict for her.

Lyra didn't really grow up in one place in Miami, seeing as how Paula dragged her to whatever dirty couch or boarded-up row house she could find in her search for her next high or next john, whichever she was fiendin' for at the time.

The brothers, Bruce and Reginald, had been standing near one of the windows in the airy room, but with all the commotion they turned to look at her. Reginald with his round face and dark eyes smiled a toothy grin, and she walked to him quickly, falling into his thick arms. "Hi, Uncle Reggie."

"Hey, Peanut. Carolyn's right, you're prettier than you were when you left."

Being the smallest of the Donovans' children when they were growing up had earned Lyra the nickname Peanut. The cousins had come up with their own nicknames for her.

"Thanks," she replied before letting her gaze settle on Bruce Donovan. Tall and broad-shouldered, his medium-brown complexion blended handsomely with the graying mustache and beard.

He reached for her and she walked easily into his embrace. Of all the Donovan men, Bruce held a special place in her heart. He'd been the only father she'd ever known, and there were nights when she'd lain awake in the pretty pink room she had upstairs and thanked God for blessing her with him.

"Hi," she said in a whisper.

"Hi to you, too, little girl." He hugged her tight, just as he had on the tarmac that day she left to go to L.A. Over the past ten years he and Janean had called and written to her regularly, sending pictures, asking if she needed anything. She'd needed them both terribly, but had refused to admit it.

"I missed you," she admitted, with her cheek rubbing against the soft cotton of his dress shirt.

"Missed you, too. You stayed away too long and I don't like that," he chastised lightly.

Pulling away she looked up into those familiar warm eyes. There was always love and understanding there, no matter what she'd done, he always looked at her the same way. "I know. But I'm back now."

With long fingers, Bruce tweaked her nose. "You bet you are. And you're staying put this time."

Lyra wasn't too sure about that, but figured it was better to keep the thought to herself. Instead she just smiled.

"What are you all standing around for? Take a seat, we're about to bless this food so we can—" Janean abruptly stopped, as her husband, Bruce, with his hands on Lyra's shoulders, turned her around to face the door that led to the kitchen.

There she was, the woman who was responsible for all that Lyra was. She still wore her church clothes, a plum-colored silk dress that hung on her marvelously mature body as if it had been cut especially for her. Her dark brown hair was pulled back into a bun and her cherublike face bore just a light sheen of makeup. Even though she was ten years older, she was even more beautiful than Lyra had remembered.

"Hi, Ms. Janean," she said, then cleared her throat because for a second she swore she sounded just like that ten-year-old girl Janean had seen at Easterntowne Elementary School.

Janean Donovan had no words, and that was saying something, since she had always been talkative and opinionated. But now she stood silent, her hands holding the handles of a pot with steam billowing upward. She took a step toward Lyra and Lyra took a step toward her. Sean stepped in and took the pot along with the potholders out of Janean's hands. She wiped them on the stone-gray apron splattered with what looked like flour.

"My baby" was what she finally whispered, lifting

her hands and clapping them against both Lyra's cheeks. "My baby's come home," she repeated, her eyes clouding with tears.

Lyra's heart pounded in her chest as her own eyes threatened to well up. "My pretty little girl all grown up."

"I really missed you," Lyra readily admitted, falling into Janean's arms, resting her head on her shoulder in a familiar gesture. Lyra couldn't even begin to remember how many times she'd cried on Janean's shoulder, how many times Janean had whispered that everything would be all right, or how many times the woman and her family had actually made everything all right.

"I really missed you, too. Don't you ever stay away that long again," she told her.

"I won't," Lyra promised, realizing at that very moment how much this family really meant to her.

"Can we eat now? I'm starving. Minister Moore preached for a solid hour today and I'm still not sure what it was about," Parker complained.

"That's because you never pay attention," Carolyn told her son as they moved around the table to take their seats. "You probably don't even know the scripture he quoted from."

"What matters is that I showed up in the first place," Parker said in his own defense.

"It'd be good if you could get something out of showing up, son," Uncle Reggie said, holding the chair for Carolyn and scooting her in before taking his own seat.

Regan laughed. "I'm surprised he showed up at all."

"Right," Savian added. "I wonder what young lady we have to thank for getting him into the house of the Lord today."

"Doesn't matter what got him there," Carolyn said. "As long as he showed up he can receive a blessing."

"That's right," Parker agreed with a nod.

"Even though I think he'd have to stay awake in order to do that," Carolyn finished. "Next time you'll know what Minister Moore's preaching about if you stop yawning and nodding off."

By then everyone was laughing and taking their seats. Everything felt like the good old days. And then the entire Donovan family joined hands as Bruce began the prayer for the family meal. Dion, who sat right beside Lyra, just as he used to all those years ago, took her hand. Lyra's fingers nervously entwined with his and her traitorous body warmed.

Everything was not like the good old days, and that's what had kept her away all those years. It was also, damn her wayward emotions, what had brought her back.

Chapter 3

She was on the dock looking out as the moonlight's illumination danced along the water in sparkling ripples. He'd known she'd be right there, staring as if she were in her own little world, just like she used to.

Tonight Dion had been ambushed with memories, and he wasn't at all surprised. Three days ago he'd found out she was coming home, even though she hadn't been the one to tell him. That little omission stung, he'd readily admit. They'd been thick as thieves as kids growing up, even though he was four years older than she. But the minute he'd realized she loved to ride bikes, jump wheelies and climb trees as much as he did, Lyra had been one of his best buddies. For as much as he could be best buddies with a girl. Sean, on the other hand, never had much time for dirt bikes and running races, playing football and wrestling until somebody's face was being ground into the dirt and they had no other choice but to cry mercy. No, as kids that was fun for him and Lyra, and they'd both enjoyed it.

Then things had changed and they'd made that one fatal mistake—or rather, he'd made that one mistake. For ten years he'd kicked himself for kissing Lyra. Now there was a part of him that was kicking himself for not doing more than kiss her.

"So I hear you're finally going to marry him, huh?" he asked when his own silence was threatening to give him ideas that would only get him in more trouble.

She turned just as a slight breeze whisked past them lifting the ends of her curly hair slightly. She wore slacks and a tank top. The coral hue of the top added a vibrant tint to her burnt-orange complexion, giving her a more alluring quality than he knew she was aiming for. Gold bangles cuffed each of her wrists, matching the gold hoops at her ears. She looked so young standing there, so vulnerable.

"Good news travels fast," she said with a shrug.

"It took you long enough to set a date. I thought you'd have gotten married as soon as you left with Stanford." Saying the man's name—even if it was only his last name—left a bitter taste in Dion's mouth, but he did it anyway. He had to prove to himself that he could say the name of the man who would now and forever hold Lyra's heart without screaming bloody murder and hurting someone in the process.

She slipped her hands into her pockets and shrugged. The act made her pert breasts rise and fall, and Dion swallowed hard. She was his little sister. He'd do well to remember that. Hadn't that been what he'd been telling himself since the day he first noticed she had said breasts in the first place?

"I didn't leave to marry him. We just left together."

Dion nodded. "Why didn't you tell me you were coming home today? The last time you emailed me you said you were looking for another job."

"I found one."

"At *Infinity?* If you wanted to work there all you had to do was let me know. You've been so hell bent on being independent, making your own way in the world, I thought I was abiding by your wishes by leaving you alone in L.A."

She smiled and it was like a sucker punch to his gut. It was taking an amazing amount of self-control for him not to get closer to her, to touch her, one more time.

"Since when have you abided by anybody's wishes but your own, Mr. Donovan?"

"There're a few people I'd go the extra mile for," he answered trying to keep this reunion as light as possible.

Dinner had been trying. She was sitting so close to him, laughing, talking with that voice that he heard in his sleep too many nights to count. Now they were standing out here in a place where they'd had so many conversations before, talking about her upcoming wedding of all things.

"I had to come back. This is where it all began, after all," she said, then turned to the side to look out at the water again. A boat filled with young party-goers passed by in the distance. Drinks were raised as the passengers waved like they knew Dion and Lyra personally. The waters along Key Biscayne were filled with cruise ships or yachts at all times of the day and night.

"You met him here that last summer when you interned at a small newspaper." It was a statement, one that had stuck in his mind since she'd told him all those years ago. "Then you left to go to L.A. with him four months later."

She nodded. "Then we broke up a year after that."

"Because he wanted more than you did," Dion added. Lyra had called him late one night needing to talk about the breakup. It had been uncomfortable for Dion, just as thinking about her with any man was. But Lyra was his closest friend and he was hers. No way was he going to let something as small as jealousy keep him from being there for her?

"He wanted it all, marriage, house, kids. I wasn't ready for that."

"But you are now?"

"We've been back together for two years now. I think I'm ready."

"You think?"

She faced him again, looked up at him like she couldn't believe he'd said that.

"I'm getting married, Dion. Do you have a problem with that?"

Did he? Hell yeah, he did. But it was his problem and nobody else's. He'd wanted Lyra for so long, and yet beat himself up about wanting her that way. His mother would definitely not be pleased and the rest of his family would no doubt frown upon him looking at Lyra this way. They'd bash him for playing with her emotions, setting out to hurt her, since that's what they assumed he did with all his female friends. They wouldn't be happy about their seeing one another. Dion knew this, and that's why he'd pushed her away ten years ago.

But if nothing else, he had to be honest with himself.

He had a huge problem with Lyra marrying someone else when he wanted her all to himself.

"If you're happy, I'm happy," he lied as smoothly as the rays of moonlight shimmered on the water, as easily as he had said it the day he told her to leave for L.A. He lied to his best friend and miraculously found it hurt even more this time than it had before.

"Good," she said with a weak smile. "Mark and I are looking for an apartment, but until then your mom wants me to stay here. I'm starting work tomorrow, so I guess I'll see you at the office."

She started to walk away like she was going to brush right past him when Dion reached out and grasped her by the elbow.

"I—" he started to say, then stopped.

"What?" she prompted.

He gritted his teeth and let the words dissipate from his mind. "I'm proud of you and all you've accomplished. You're a great photographer and you've become a beautiful woman," he said honestly.

Her smile was genuine, touching her brown eyes the way he remembered it did when they'd been laughing together as teenagers. "Thanks, Dion. That means a lot to me. Good night."

"Good night," he said reluctantly, letting her walk away. Again.

"Where am I supposed to live?" Paula Anderson asked with one bony arm propped on an even slimmer hip.

Lyra sighed, not wanting to go through this again. She didn't need this aggravation on her first day of a new job. She was sick and tired of dealing with her mother's selfishness and irresponsibility. Immediately, guilt washed over her and she closed her eyes, counted to five and then reopened them.

"You can get a job," she said slowly. "I've given you all the money I can. I just moved across the country. Don't you realize how expensive that is?"

"Girl, don't give me that BS. And don't forget I know who you really are. Now you might think you're all high and mighty, out there foolin' those rich folk, but you ain't any better than I am."

After years of hearing the same story, it was a wonder Lyra had any pride, or self-confidence for that matter. But she did, and she owed that to the upbringing of Janean Donovan.

"I don't have any money."

"You got money. I know they probably got an account set up for you and everything. That woman's been so in love with my child for years. It's a damn shame. Got kids of her own but still gotta go out and try to steal somebody else's."

"Well, if somebody else had been taking care of their child, maybe another woman wouldn't have to." Lyra's reply was quick, her reflexes even quicker as she caught Paula's long narrow fingers just as she tried to slap her across the cheek.

"I told you not to put your hands on me again," she said with carefully tempered anger.

"And I told you not to forget who birthed you."

They were locked in a stare-down, something that had happened too many times before. Paula wanted Lyra to bend to her will, to do whatever she said, whenever she said it. Lyra wanted Paula to get a damned clue.

She was a grown woman and long over her mother's drug-addicted ways and bitterness.

Sadly, none of that meant Lyra didn't love her mother. After all, this was the woman who gave birth to her and for a little while the woman who'd taken care of her. Then one day everything just went totally wrong. They were kicked out of their small apartment with only the clothes on their backs, so Paula had to do what was necessary to make sure her baby ate, at least that's the reason she gave Lyra for turning tricks in dark alleys while Lyra kept watch on the corner. But that was then. Over the years Lyra had become adept at leaving her past where it belonged, in the past.

"I'm not giving you any money. You know how to take care of yourself," Lyra answered seriously and turned to walk away.

Paula had cut her off just as she was about to walk into the Excalibur Business Center that was owned by the Donovans, the headquarters of *Infinity* as well as DNM—Donovan Network Management. Now, Lyra wanted to get inside as quickly as possible. It was a secure building, she knew. Nobody was getting onto that elevator and upstairs without an ID badge or a phone call from the building's security. Paula didn't want to see any of the Donovans, that was for sure. Their relationship was not good, never had been, no matter how much Janean had tried.

"Don't walk away from me, gal," Paula said. Her Southern drawl usually came out when she was drunk or high—or some combination of the two—and when she was pissed off, which by now, Lyra knew she was.

A long time ago, Paula would ask Lyra for money— beg a little, cry for a couple minutes, and then Lyra would give her what she wanted. Then there'd be sloppy kisses, empty promises and quick goodbyes—a routine Lyra had grown to despise. But Lyra was done with that. If she counted the money she'd given her mother over the years, it would easily amount to a few thousand dollars. And that was nothing compared to all the money the Donovans had given her to stay away and leave Lyra with them. So part of the debt she owed this family was her mother's. The other part was her own, and she was ready to start repaying it.

"Don't threaten me, Paula. We've been there and done that. I'd think by now you'd know the limits."

"You sure got a smart mouth. I bet if I come over there and smack the taste out of it, you'll know who's boss."

The bright morning sunshine glittered over Paula's fiery red hair, which was shaved close like a man's. Leopard-print pants looked as if they were painted on her slim legs while the black shirt she wore slipped off one shoulder and hung loosely over a boyishly flat chest. She looked like she could have been about twelve years old. And if there had been a strong wind, she'd fall right over. A brief pang of regret touched Lyra's heart at the sight.

"But that's not going to happen now is it?" a masculine voice said.

Both their heads turned as Dion approached. Lyra instantly wanted to disappear. She hated for Dion to see her mother like this, to be reminded of where she came from.

"Well, looky here." Paula tried to whistle but her two front teeth were missing so the sound was empty and produced more spittle than air. "You done growed up, boy."

Dion only nodded at Paula then looked to Lyra. "Go into the building," he told her. He could be such an arrogant ass at times. And other times he could be her savior. That was a role Dion always loved playing. Still, he should have known better than to think she'd just obey him.

"I've got this under control," she said.

"No. I'll handle it," he countered.

"You her shining knight?" Paula asked, her speech slurring even more as she stumbled toward Dion.

Lyra rolled her eyes. Dion reached out a hand to catch Paula as she leaned into him but nearly missed him entirely. "I'll call you a cab, Paula. Then you need to disappear. For good," he said with a finality that made Lyra quietly gasp.

He was right, her mother needed to go. This was her job, her new life. She didn't need or want her here.

"I ain't goin' nowhere," Paula said straightening herself up and flattening her palms on Dion's chest.

He wore a suit today, a gray double-breasted Armani—Dion loved just about anything Armani—with a crisp white shirt and bold peach tie with tiny flecks of silver. The sight of her mother's slim hands, bony wrists and veiny arms on him made her stomach churn.

Lyra stepped over, clasping her mother by the waist and pulling her away. "Just go, Paula. I'll call you later."

She didn't miss Dion's frown at her words, but chose to ignore them.

"I'll leave when I get what I came for," Paula huffed.

Lyra rolled her eyes skyward. This was not the way she wanted to start her first day at *Infinity*. Hell, it wasn't the way she wanted to live her life. But silly her for thinking she had any control of that. "Here," she said digging into the side zipper of her purse and pulling out the cash she'd stuffed there yesterday after tipping the cab driver who'd picked her up at the airport. "Just take it and go."

Paula fingered the money and looked up at Lyra with a frown. "You call me later," she said, then looked over at Dion. "You still sharp, boy—sharp as a tack. That's why that girl's trying to get you to put a ring on it." Throwing her head back Paula laughed as she sashayed her pitiful backside out of the parking lot.

"She's still guilting you into giving her drug money," Dion said from behind as Lyra rubbed her fingers against her temples.

"This is an old conversation," she said. Taking a deep breath she turned around and walked right up to Dion. "It's not your concern. I can handle my mother."

Dion nodded and fell into step beside her, heading to the double glass doors of the building. "By giving her whatever she wants so she'll leave you alone. That's a good way to handle her. It's like feeding a stray cat because you don't want to see it starve. It's going to keep coming back, Lyra. I know you know all this already."

Lyra reached for the door and yanked it open. "Then why do you insist on saying it over and over again?" she said, glancing over her shoulder before walking through.

Dion followed her inside. "Because you never listen," he mumbled through clenched teeth. "She's never going to leave you alone until you make her."

Spinning around to quickly face him she asked, "And

just how do I do that? How do I turn my back on the only family I have, Dion?"

He stopped cold, looking her dead in the eye. Then his voice lowered. "I thought we were your family."

Lyra sighed. This was how this conversation always went with them. Dion told her what to do, she argued about it, then he made her feel like crap because deep down she knew he was right. "You don't understand," she said finally. "I just want to move on. I just want to do my job and live my life without all these problems clouding it."

Dion started walking ahead, waving at the two guards who manned the front desk. Lyra followed behind him, waving at the guards, as well. They'd let her in because she was with him. Later today they'd get a memo from human resources with her name, a photo ID and the department she worked in. Tomorrow morning when she walked in alone, they'd smile and greet her just as they had Dion. That's how it worked in the world of the Donovans, a world she'd tiptoed around in for most of her life.

"You don't want problems, then deal with them, Lyra. Stop acting like the victim here, because you're not."

They were in the elevator now, a seething Dion standing beside her, briefcase clasped in both hands in front of him. She could smell his cologne, felt the waves of warmth as his scent wafted to her nose, down the back of her throat, into her chest, and downward until she was completely full of him.

"Stop acting like an asshole, Dion. Oh, I forgot, you can't help that."

He chuckled. "Calling me names isn't going to solve your problem."

"Oh, yeah? Well, since you know so much, tell me what is going to solve my problem?"

"Grow a backbone," he said just as the elevator dinged and the doors opened. "Until then Paula and needy people just like her are going to walk all over you every time."

He stepped off the elevator and Lyra wanted nothing more than to follow him and keep the argument going, but that would be futile. She was always the one to get upset, to yell and scream and develop a mega headache trying to prove her point to Dion Donovan. And he was the one who kept a cool head, a sarcastic tone and deflected each and every argument she came up with. Some things never changed.

Chapter 4

"Tomorrow is the Vina Vanell shoot. She's on the October cover with a feature story that coincides with the release of her new CD."

"And she just announced her engagement and confirmed her baby bump with rapper Jride," Lyra finished Regan's sentence typing notes into the calendar on her iPad.

Regan was an editor at *Infinity*. She mainly focused on the celebrity aspect of the magazine, leaving the business profiles and features to her brother Savian. Regan had always loved the glitz and glamour of Hollywood growing up. Lyra remembered spending endless nights at her house, where they dressed in all Regan's pretty gowns and pretended they were walking the red carpet. Lyra always hated that, standing and posing, smiling and gesturing. She would've much rather been on the sidelines with the paparazzi getting the perfect shot, not arriving in a limo and wearing a designer dress.

"You know about that, huh?" Regan asked, crossing one long, evenly tanned leg over the other, showing off another one of her passions, shoes. They were platforms, copper and black in a lace print with five-inch heels that only added to Regan's already-tall stature.

"I hear things," Lyra said with a smile.

They were in her office. She had an office, Lyra thought with an inward smile. In L.A. she'd been working for Jacque Landow, one of the best-known photographers around. Then Mark had gotten the job offer in Miami and announced he was coming back home, about ten seconds after he asked her to marry him. A twinge of nervous energy slid over her and she sat up in her chair, focusing more on the calendar than she needed to.

"Then Friday there's the Heat game. They're in the NBA Finals, so getting good shots of the Big Three is crucial."

"Right," Regan said nodding. "And next Saturday's the gala. Have you gotten a dress yet? Probably not. I know how you hate shopping, even though I'm loving that blouse you're wearing. I have the coolest royal blue mini that would be perfect with it, because those pants aren't doing a damned thing for you."

That was Regan, too, the fashion guru, and forever trying to be a stylist for Lyra.

"I like what I'm wearing. It's comfortable and professional so it works just fine."

"If you're a nun," Regan joked.

Lyra didn't laugh but did look down at her gray Ann Taylor low-ride pants and sensible black pumps. Her top was a crisp white button-down with sleeves she'd folded because they were too long and she hated when her clothes interfered with her photography. She'd taken only a few shots this morning after Dion had left her at the elevator. The shots were mostly of the office, no one in particular, just things that caught her eye. She'd been eager to feel the camera in her hands, to hear the click of the shutter capturing a moment in time.

"I like my outfit," she murmured again.

"Of course you do. So listen, what about the wedding? When's the big day? And what are we wearing? I'm putting in my bid right now for fuchsia. I look great in pinks."

Lyra had to smile at that. Regan Lorae Donovan looked great in a dirty lamp shade and wrinkled sheet. She was a classic beauty, not stunning or striking, but still good-looking. On the other hand, Lyra saw herself as cute, not plain Jane or someone to write home about, but reasonably attractive. When she stood next to Regan, Lyra figured her cuteness was ratcheted up a couple notches, but that wasn't something she strived for. Being in the spotlight was not important to Lyra.

"Not sure," she answered glibly, and knew in that instant she'd said the wrong thing.

"What do you mean 'not sure'?" Not sure about the date or not sure about marrying Mark?"

Now Lyra had two options—she could lie and say she was simply not sure about the date and Regan would immediately know she was lying. She'd push even harder to get the truth. Or she could simply fess up and finally confide everything that had been weighing on her mind.

"Both. Kind of..." She sat back in the chair and

waited for Regan's barrage of questions that surprisingly didn't come.

"You don't want to marry him."

It was a statement, not a question.

"You've been with him off and on for around nine years, but you don't want to marry him?" Regan continued.

"You make it sound so awful, like I'm a terrible person or something. I'm just a little undecided."

Regan nodded, tapping a finger to her chin and pursing her frosted lips. "Let's just add up the pros of Mark Stanford. He's damned fine, and I mean fine with a capital *F*. He's now CEO for one of the fastest-growing social-media sites, so he's hella rich. He knows everyone that is anyone and he's crazy about you."

"And the cons?" Lyra asked hoping Regan could come up with more than Lyra had.

"Hmm." She thought for a minute, her chin-length chestnut hair moving slightly as she tilted her head. "He drives a Hummer, which is by far one of the ugliest SUVs I've ever seen."

Lyra erupted with laughter, which led to Regan doing the same until they were both almost in tears. Leave it to Regan to make her laugh when she was really down.

Taking a deep breath Lyra finally confided, "I just don't know that I'm ready to marry him. Like, I know that one day I want to be married and to spend the rest of my life with the man of my dreams—or at least a man that I'm madly in love with. But I don't know that it's Mark. Do you understand that?"

Regan nodded. "I do. So what now? Are you going to tell him or go through with it because you think it's the right thing to do? I know how you are. If you think you're going against some unwritten rule or some non-sense, you'll walk on hot coals or cut off your own hand."

"Ever the drama queen," Lyra said, just as her cell phone rang. She looked down at it and frowned. "It's Mark."

Regan nodded and stood. "And I'm leaving."

"Go ahead and bail on me. That's what you always do," she whined.

"This is your pity party, and you're about to be a run-away bride. You can catch me up later when we have dinner. I already made reservations for seven. Don't be late, and change your clothes, please."

Lyra waved Regan out of her office just as she answered the cell phone. "Hey, Mark."

"Hey, sweetheart. Just wanted to check and see how everything was going on your first day."

Mark was very considerate.

"Oh, it's going fine. I was just meeting with Regan, going over the upcoming shoots and deadlines. I have to go to Friday's game, and I'm doing a shoot tomorrow, so I'll be pretty tied up this week," she said, just in case he wanted to get together to talk about the wedding. For a guy, Mark was very excited about planning a big, lavish wedding. A little too excited.

"Okay. Well, I guess if you have to work. I wanted to go over to my parents' and get started on some of the wedding plans."

Lyra knew him like she knew each line in the palm of her hand. It wasn't hard though, by the end of the month Mark's new assistant would probably know him just as well. And yet she still felt closer to Dion.

"Sorry."

"No, don't be. I understand this is your career. But don't make any plans for next Saturday. My mom wants us to come over for dinner."

Lyra groaned. "The Donovans are having their annual Wish Upon a Star charity ball that Saturday. All the family is expected to be there."

There was a pause on the phone, and Lyra knew that Mark was thinking she wasn't really a member of the Donovan family, although he'd never say that to her. While they'd been in L.A., he'd constantly reminded her that the Donovans were not blood, that what Janean did was out of charity and that it was time she lived her life without clinging to them.

"You haven't been there for the past ten years. I'm sure they won't miss you for one more," he argued.

"The difference is I'm staying in their house now. They'll expect me to be there."

"And that's another thing. We can get an apartment until we find a house. You don't have to stay with them."

"I know that, Mark. I can get my own apartment for that matter. But it means a lot to Janean that I spend some time with them after being away for so long."

"I'm starting to feel like your mother where the Donovans are concerned. It's just not healthy the way they're attached to you and you to them. You don't belong."

"And just where do I belong?" she asked, as the headache that had been a dull pain after her argument with Dion began to ramp up a notch.

"Calm down, sweetie. Listen to what I'm trying to say. You and I come from regular families who go out and work hard to make a way for themselves. We're not from money and privilege."

"But your salary just made you a millionaire before

your thirtieth birthday. That doesn't exactly make you a 'regular' guy."

"That's money I earned, Lyra. Not money that was given to me. It's different. They're different. And you shouldn't spend your time trying to fit in with them."

His words hurt, mainly because she'd been telling herself that most of her life. She knew the Donovans were different, knew that they weren't part of her family. So she didn't need Mark to remind her of that fact.

"Go to dinner at your mother's on Saturday and give her my apologies. I won't be there."

"Wait," Mark said hastily. "Don't hang up angry. I don't want us to fight, not about this anyway. I'll take you to the charity ball, and on Sunday we'll spend the day with my parents. Okay?"

Lyra was quiet. Her elbows were propped up on her desk and she began to wonder why she didn't just end things with Mark. "Fine," she said with a sigh. Because it was just like Dion had said, she needed to grow a backbone.

"What's on your mind?" Sean asked the moment he stepped into Dion's office and closed the door.

Dion looked up from his desk then stared down at the Rolex on his left wrist. "Meeting's not for another fifteen minutes."

Sean nodded walking closer to the desk and taking a seat in one of the guest chairs. "That's why I came early to ask you what's going on?"

Spreading his palms on the desk, it was apparent to Dion that Sean had something on his mind. He realized that he wasn't going to get to finish reading the distribution reports he'd just received from Sean's assistant.

"Why don't you tell me what you think is going on, because I'm sure you have some little idea roaming around in that head of yours," Dion said, sitting back in his chair and looking directly at his brother.

They were close, almost like twins but not. They even looked alike—they were both tall with slim, muscular builds, and they both had the same caramel complexion that their mother had. Sean was the studious brother with runway-model looks, a square jawline and a cleft chin, and dreamy eyes that girls loved to stare into. Dion almost laughed as he remembered back in high school girls said exactly that about his younger brother. On the other hand, he was the athletic one with rugged good looks and a bad-boy image that made him attractive to a totally different type of girl. Still, there was no denying that the Donovan men were just as attractive and just as unattainable as their cousins in Las Vegas.

"Lyra's downstairs with Regan. I hear she's got her assignments and plans on hitting the ground running."

Dion rubbed his chin. "That's a good thing, right?"

"It's a very good thing for *Infinity,* since Lyra's a phenomenal photographer. We're more than lucky to have her on board, and it's good for Lyra because I think she missed being around family."

"So it's a win-win all around."

"I think you know that," Sean suggested.

"Just spit it out, man," Dion said.

"Okay, since you want me to spell it out," Sean said with a frown. "Mom says she's talking about getting married later in the year, to that internet company guy."

"I know. His name's Mark."

"He's the one she left to go to L.A. with."

Dion nodded. "The one and only."

"And now they're back and getting married."

"You're wasting time going over facts we already know."

"Then how about we talk about the one we both keep skirting around?"

"And what's that?"

"You don't like Mark whatever his name is. You don't want Lyra to marry him."

Dion sighed. "Sean. Don't do this."

"Don't say what you're thinking. Who the hell is this guy and what are his real intentions toward Lyra?"

"They've been together for years. She knows what she's doing."

"Really? You think so? Because from what I saw of her last night, she looks like she's undecided."

Now that had Dion's attention. "I didn't see that."

"Because you were too busy trying to ignore her, which I don't really understand at the moment. Each time Mom asked her about the plans for the wedding she clammed up. When Regan asked her when they were going shopping for dresses, she changed the subject. What woman do you know isn't ecstatic about planning their wedding and ready to talk about the preparations until they're blue in the face?"

Sean had a point. One that Dion hadn't considered because he didn't want to hear about Lyra's wedding plans any more than Lyra wanted to talk about them. He'd never liked Stanford, the internet guy, and disliked him even more for taking Lyra away and convincing her to marry him. But that was his issue, not Sean's.

"Look, Lyra's a grown woman. She can make her own decisions."

"What if she's not seeing things clearly? You know how women can be. Don't you think, as her brothers, we at least owe it to her to check things out, make sure she's making the right decision?"

No. Oh, God, no. Because if Dion found out Stanford didn't have Lyra's best interests at heart, he'd kill that bastard. He only needed one more excuse to beat that pompous wannabe to a pulp.

"I don't want to interfere. Besides, Lyra's got bigger problems than that."

"Like what?"

"Paula's back."

Sean pinched the bridge of his nose, something he often did when he was stressed. "God, why can't that woman just disappear? Haven't we given her enough money to do that?"

"You know money for people like her is another kind of drug. Every time she gets a little she needs more. I told Lyra to stop enabling her."

"And what'd she say?"

"She told me it's her mother, just like she always does."

"It's a pity she's still holding on to that tiny shred of hope. So you don't want to do anything about Mark and we're supposed to sit back and let her mother hold her hostage for money day in and day out. Is that your plan?"

Dion thought about it a minute. There was a limit to what he wanted to tell Sean, because the last thing he wanted was to involve his brother. But he'd considered what his brother had said, and had thought about nothing else all morning.

"I'll deal with Paula."

"And Mark?"

"I have a feeling he's going to trip up sooner or later. Lyra may be foolish for falling into her mother's trap, but she's not a fool when it comes to men. She knows what she wants and what she doesn't. She'll make the right decision when the time comes."

Dion hoped like hell his words were true, because he didn't know if he could stop himself from standing up and objecting when the preacher said, "Speak now or forever hold your peace."

There was a knock at his door and they both acknowledged the meeting was about to begin. Sean cleared his throat and straightened his tie.

"I'll follow your lead on this, but know that I'm still worried about her," he said.

Dion tried to disregard his brother's concerns. "You worry about everything, man. Chill out a little. It'll do you some good." It would do them both some good, because if Sean was worried then that was not a good thing.

Chapter 5

Lyra preferred digital to manually operated cameras. A lot of photographers did nowadays. She didn't miss the sound of the 35mm, but her heart almost always skipped a beat with the nearly inaudible click of her Nikon D3S. It was one of her favorites because of its expanded buffer and its continuous high-speed frame capability.

That's exactly what she needed today to capture the moody and eccentric sultry neo-soul singer Vina Vanell. Vina moved at her own pace in her own little world, no matter how many directions Lyra gave her. Between her stylists and makeup artists and whoever else was in her entourage, she occasionally offered a look or a gesture that was worth snapping.

Vina Vanell had risen to the top of the charts with her soulful debut release a year ago. Now her photo was on every tabloid front page and her songs were remixed by practically every deejay. Her love life had also taken off on the gossip pages when she left her no name manager and begin a tumultuous affair with the marijuana-smoking, DUI-plagued, newest rapper on the hip hop scene—Jride. To say they were the perfect couple was comical. Vina was twelve years older than Jride, and her music appealed to slightly older fans of R&B, in sharp contrast to Jride's thuggish crowd.

But none of that was Lyra's concern. All she needed to do was get the perfect shots to go with the story.

"Something by the window would be nice," she heard herself say, but didn't hold out hope that it would happen.

Vina wore a white bodysuit with leopard print thigh-high boots that gave a significant boost to her five-foot-six stature so that she stood almost six feet tall. The long, glossy flowing mane of blond hair cascaded down her back as her lavishly jeweled eyelashes winked at every turn. She looked like a circus act that was just barely tame. Her boyfriend, Jride, hovered in the corner with a cell phone in one ear and a diamond stud as big as Lyra's eyeball in the other. She had to refrain from rolling her eyes at the wasteful and ostentatious display of money. Her job was to take pictures, not pass judgment.

"Okay," she said finally. "I think I have what I need." And if she didn't, there was always Photoshop.

"Ms. Vanell wants to do a wardrobe change," the skinny little assistant with two cell phones in her hand and the too-tight fake ponytail said without even looking at Lyra.

"Not today. I have what I need."

"She wants to see the photos before they run," she added.

"I'll make sure that happens," Lyra quipped. *When hell freezes over,* she thought.

Packing up her stuff, she was happier than she'd been in the past few weeks as she left the studio, stepped into the elevator and was heading as far away from Vina Vanell and her entourage as she could get. Her cell phone rang the minute she'd stepped off the elevator facing the fading light of late afternoon.

"Lyra Anderson," she answered.

"Hello, Lyra Anderson. This is Dion Donovan calling to see if you're hungry."

She couldn't help but smile. "Of course I'm hungry. I just finished the most grueling shoot you could imagine."

"What? You mean with Vina Vanell? She's a doll."

"If you're a six-feet-plus-tall man with eyes only for her, I guess she might be. For me, she was a pain in the ass."

Dion laughed. Lyra did, too, as she walked to her car. It felt good.

"So how about some barbecue from Shorty's?"

"Now you know I'm not about to turn that down. I can be there in about forty minutes."

"Cool. I'm just leaving the office, so it'll take me about that long to get there, too. Drive carefully," he said before hanging up.

"Yes, Dad," Lyra said with a smirk before opening her trunk and putting her equipment inside. No matter how old she was Dion would always treat her like his little sister. Even after their kiss ten years ago, the kiss that still haunted Lyra's dreams.

As she got behind the wheel and started up her car, Lyra let her mind wander back to the time when she was young and Dion was young and they were both into exploring what feelings might be between them, or at least she'd been into exploring her feelings. The jury was still out on what Dion had been thinking that day.

It had been Lyra's senior prom and Dion's senior year at Columbia. He'd come home early, since the last couple of months of the semester were a free ride for him, as he'd completed all his requirements early so that all he had to do was wait for his graduation day. Mark had taken her to the prom, since they'd met the summer before. If she hadn't met Mark, Lyra probably wouldn't have even gone to the prom. Parties, flashy clothes and stupid high school activities weren't really her thing. But Mark had insisted, he'd sworn she'd regret not going for the rest of her life if she missed her senior prom.

Well, as it turned out, the music sucked, the food was bad and everybody already knew who the prom king and queen were going to be—Regan Donovan and Joshua Lang. All of the Donovan children went to public school, despite the money and prestige the family had. The Donovans still had a down-to-earth sensibility that reflected their good upbringing and compassion for those less fortunate. So while Regan had been ecstatic about prom, Lyra had just gone along for the ride. A ride that was as boring as the last cycle on the merry-go-round before the carnival closed.

She'd insisted Mark take her right home, foregoing the after parties, including the one Regan was throwing at the Ritz-Carlton. She just wasn't in the mood to party. In fact, she hadn't been in the mood for much lately, her mind had been on something else—more like someone else.

Dion had come home that Christmas and stayed until the first of February. In that time she'd felt differently about him. Of course, he'd changed since he'd been away at college. He was older, and had settled down as much as Dion could settle down. He was definitely the partier of the Donovan boys and took every opportunity he could to have a damn good time. His brother, Sean, studied and worked his butt off his first year at Columbia.

But that wasn't the only change. It seemed, at least to Lyra, that Dion looked different. His cocoa-brown eyes seemed darker, more intriguing, and his body had morphed from a tall and slightly built physique to that of a tall, muscular Adonis. She'd caught him coming out of the bathroom after a shower one morning with a towel wrapped around his hips and her entire body had gone haywire. Her seventeen-year-old breasts had ached in the tiny B-cup bra she wore, while the juncture between her legs throbbed incessantly. Her mouth had gone dry instantly so that she'd barely been able to mutter good morning before half running down the hall to the safety of her own room. It had been terribly embarrassing, at least for her.

She'd fought off Mark's sexual advances for the billionth time since they'd been dating. No, it wasn't anything inappropriate considering they were healthy teenagers. She just hadn't been in the mood to kiss him or be touched by him and that was most likely due to the fact that she wanted desperately to be kissed and touched by someone else.

The minute she'd let herself into the house she'd been nearly startled to death when he spoke.

"Early night?"

Clutching her chest she spun around barely making out the outline of his face in the dimly lit foyer. "Crap! What are you doing lurking around in the dark?"

"Waiting for the girls to come in from their night of partying. I see you're the first to make it home. You okay?" he asked, taking a step closer to her so that she could see the tank top he usually wore when he worked out and the basketball shorts that grazed his knees.

"Yeah, I'm home, so you can stand down now," she said, pushing past him and heading for the kitchen.

But he grabbed her arm making her exit difficult. "Wait a minute. How was the prom? Did you have fun?"

Lyra sighed. "No, it wasn't fun, but I didn't expect it to be." Her entire arm had become warm from his touch, so she squirmed until he let her go.

"Stanford not an ideal date, huh?"

Lyra shrugged. "He was what he was supposed to be, I guess. I just didn't want to go in the first place."

"I know you don't like dressing up," he said while reaching out a hand and lifting the skirt of the knee-length taffeta dress she wore. "But you look really nice."

Something about the way his voice dipped when he said that had her heart pounding. She didn't know what to say or do so she just stood there looking at him, wanting him.

"So you and this guy getting serious?"

Lyra cleared her throat. "I don't know." And she really didn't. She didn't want to consider getting serious with any guy right now, especially since Mark wasn't the guy she really liked.

She wanted Dion Donovan, and she knew she shouldn't. He was off-limits. Try telling that to her body.

"Do you want to be serious with him?"

"Do you want to be serious with Tish Hamilton?" she countered. Dion's flavor of the month was Tish, daughter of Congressman Lloyd Hamilton. Or at least she was the flavor when Dion was home. While he was away at school he had an array of other flavors that Tish, in all her naive stupidity, didn't know about.

He smiled. The corner of his mouth lifted and his eyes gleamed, which meant that what she'd said amused him. Lately, it seemed he gave her that look a lot.

Now it was his turn to shrug. "You know how it is."

"No. Why don't you tell me?"

"She's just here every time I come home—nothing real serious. Just someone to hang out with."

"So that's all you're doing, is hanging out with her? She and her mother are already picking out her wedding gown."

His fingers still played with her dress and he stood a little too close for her comfort.

"That's not my problem. I've never made her any promises."

"But you haven't told her she's a convenience, either?"

"Nah, I haven't." He chuckled. "But I was asking about you and Stanford. He's your boyfriend, right?"

Lyra folded her arms over her chest because she didn't know what else to do with them. "I guess."

"Did you let him kiss you tonight?"

The question startled her, and Lyra took a step back until Dion could no longer toy with her dress and his scent could no longer assault her senses. Clearing her throat, she finally stammered, "That's n-none of your business."

"Come on, Lyra. We don't keep secrets. I can tell you any and everything, and you can trust me to do the same. We've always been like that."

He was right. Even thoughts she couldn't share with Regan, who was the same age as she was, Lyra could share with Dion. It had been like that for so long she could barely remember when they weren't there for each other. Tonight, however, it just seemed different.

"I didn't want him to kiss me," she whispered.

Dion moved closer again. "Why?"

She was looking into his eyes now, eyes that were normally laughing or at least friendly. Tonight they seemed darker, more entrancing. He kept his gaze locked on hers as he stepped closer to her. She continued to retreat until the banister jabbing into her spine stopped her.

"Why what?" She swallowed because her throat was suddenly very dry.

"Why didn't you want him to kiss you?"

"I just didn't," she answered breathily. His chest, the hard ridges of carefully maintained muscle, pressed against her body.

"He should have kissed you," Dion said, his voice getting lower.

This was crazy. Why was Dion pressed against her this way? And why was her body reacting to it? Her arms and fingers tingled and wanted to wrap around him, touch him and feel him. Thoughts were swimming around in her head until breathing was becoming a chore.

"No. I didn't want to kiss him."

"Who do you want to kiss?" he asked.

Lyra closed her eyes.

She wanted his kiss, Dion's—the one person who had vowed to protect her like a big brother all her life. She wanted his familiar lips on hers—the same lips that had shared numerous fudge pops with her because they were their favorites.

"I—" She couldn't speak, couldn't tell him in words. Then again, she didn't need to. Dion and Lyra had always had a close relationship, from the moment she'd first set foot into the Donovan house. She'd related to him even more so than to his mother, who had brought her home. They were always in tune with each other. Now was no different.

Dion's hand snaked around her neck and tilted her head while dipping his head closer—so close his breath grazed her lips.

"Do you want me to kiss you, Lyra?"

Her mind screamed no! But her body melded against his in defiance, her hands going to his biceps where her fingers dug in and held on tight. "Yes," she whispered, and then one of her many dreams about Dion came true.

As her eyes fluttered shut and fireworks exploded inside her head, Dion's lips touched hers with a soft sweep. Then both his hands were cupping her face, pulling her closer. She stood on tiptoe to reach him as his lips slanted over hers again. When his tongue swiped over her sensitive skin Lyra gasped, opening her mouth to him. His tongue was quick and experienced, sweeping inside and coaxing hers to join in the game. With long swishing motions he lavished her mouth. His hard body pressed hers painfully into the banister, but the pain was muted by the stark pleasure of his kiss and his touch.

This was by far the best part of her senior prom and Lyra wanted the moment to last forever, wanted this kiss to go on and on until she could see and breathe nothing and no one else but Dion.

But it wasn't meant to be.

Dion pulled back abruptly staring down at her as if she'd just grown two heads. His hands dropped to his sides and he backed away.

She stood there like an idiot because her feet wouldn't allow her to do anything else.

"Sorry," he mumbled as he continued to back away. He was moving past her through the double doors that led down another hall and to the kitchen before she could respond, which was a good thing because even ten years later, Lyra had no idea what her response would have been.

What she did know now was that she was still in love with Dion Donovan. She still wanted his touch and his kiss just as badly as she had that night she stood in the foyer as the naive high school senior. And she was still in just as much denial about it as she was then.

Chapter 6

When they were seated at a table with the same chairs and tables as the last time she was here, Lyra picked up the menu and read it like she didn't have a clue what was on it. Across the table from her, Dion did the same, then ordered two glasses of water and two Cokes.

"So how was the shoot?" he asked.

"I think I got some pretty good shots, with no help from Vina, though. Why didn't you warn me how difficult she was?"

"Figured you'd read that much in the tabloids."

"Nobody believes those things. But I guess in this case they may be partly true. Did I tell you she slapped her assistant twice? The poor girl didn't know whether she was coming or going after that last hit and the rest of her entourage just looked away like it was something that happened daily."

Dion shook his head. "It probably is. It's a shame what people will do for money."

"Yeah," Lyra said, wondering if he was referring to the diva Vina or her mother. Paula was a sore subject between them, always had been.

Janean Donovan had come to an elementary school play at a school that one of their foundations was donating money to, and she'd seen ten-year-old Lyra cleaning up the stage after the play. Lyra remembered with startling clarity how embarrassed she was when the impeccably dressed woman with the big smile and large bright jewelry had spoken to her. Since mostly all the students had already gone home with their parents, Janean was confused as to why Lyra was still there. Lyra never told her that she spent a lot of nights locked in the janitor's closet waiting for school the next day to avoid having to return to the one-bedroom apartment where her mother was either passed out or entertaining company. But somehow she figured Janean already knew.

"I hate people like her. You know, ones that have a lot, but don't know what to do with it or appreciate it. They just make me sick."

Dion rubbed a hand over his chin. "I agree."

"What's up with you?" she asked, putting her menu down finally. "You look like you've got something on your mind."

His fingers froze, and his hand dropped from his face. "No. I don't. Just thought you needed a pick-me-up after a long day."

She nodded, not believing him for one minute. "And how was your day?"

"Work is work, you know that," he said, nonchalantly. Something was definitely bothering him.

"*Infinity*'s doing great. Back in L.A. there was lots of buzz about it expanding internationally. Are you working on that?"

Dion drank a little of his water and replied, "We had a meeting about distribution yesterday. It's looking good. We're also talking about launching a program based on the magazine on DNT. We'd continue with the fashion highlights and entertainment news, and expand our entrepreneurs spotlight section a bit. Sean has some great ideas and so does Regan. Savian's a little reserved about the move, though."

"Savian's a little reserved about everything," Lyra said with a light chuckle. "But it sounds like a great idea. On the fashion side, you know I had a chance to meet your cousin Adam's wife, Camille. CK Davis Designs is getting a lot of attention from Hollywood stars. What do you think about maybe doing a spotlight on her? Maybe DNT could develop a reality show around a designer's life. I mean, she started her company and has grown it into something spectacular. All the stylists in L.A. have her on speed dial now."

Dion watched her as she talked. He'd missed their conversations over the years while she'd been away. Sure, they wrote to each other and talked on the phone every once in a while. Their text messages were much more frequent. But none of that gave him as much satisfaction as sitting here looking into her deep brown eyes and hearing her voice in person.

"Have you been eavesdropping on my private meetings, Ms. Anderson?" he asked with a smile. "Sean and I have been tossing around some of those ideas for months. We were all just out in Vegas for the dedication ceremony for Adam and Camille's baby. That's when the idea first hit us. With all the reality shows getting huge ratings, we figured this would be a good time for DNT to take the plunge."

"Then great minds must think alike." She smiled at him as the waitress came to take their order. "I'll have the pork, potato salad and baked beans."

The tiny waitress nodded as she scribbled on her pad. "What kind of sauce?"

Dion answered for her. "Sweet, and put the bread on the side."

Lyra smiled at him again. He loved when she did that, when her face lit up with happiness that made her eyes sparkle. He especially loved the fact that it was all for him. At least for now, he'd been the one to make that sparkle appear, to make her happy.

"How do you still remember what I like to eat?" she said.

"I remember everything about you, Lyra." And that was the honest truth. It didn't matter how long she'd been away, there wasn't any detail he didn't remember about her. Everything about Lyra was etched in his mind, as if losing even one minor detail would somehow mean losing her.

He placed his order and the food arrived quickly. The conversation once again settled on *Infinity* and plans for the future.

"I'd like you to cover Fashion Week in New York in the fall, then travel to London, Milan and Paris. We're planning a special issue and want lots of great photos. Of course, Regan will go with you to interview the designers."

"Camille will no doubt be there."

"I know, and we'll include her in the feature. Hopefully by that time we'll have met with her and her reps, and development for a reality show or a series in the magazine or on the network will be ready to announce. Sean's keeping in touch with Adam to see when Camille will be ready to start taking meetings."

"You're sure you want me to do the entire Fashion Week shoot?" she asked, a little uneasy about the assignment.

He took a bite of his ribs, marveling in the taste of the spicy sauce. After swallowing, he wiped his fingers and replied, "What kind of question is that? Of course I want you to handle it."

"I'm just saying that I'm the newest photographer on staff. Don't you think it'll look bad, you giving me all the plum assignments?"

"No. I think it'll look smart, me giving you all the choice assignments. Look, *Infinity* is more than just my job. You, of all people should know that. It's a part of my father's legacy. It's up to us to make this as good as the rest of the Donovan enterprises. I'm not about to take any chances with that. The fact that you're family has nothing to do with how good you are, or how highly sought-after you're becoming. Hell, we'll be lucky if in five years the magazine can afford to keep you."

"All right, all right, you don't have to go overboard," she said, laughing. "I was just asking. You know I don't want any special treatment."

"And believe me, you're not going to get any. Those pics better be good enough for the cover or you're going to have to go to Vina's house to take some more."

"Argghhh. Please don't threaten me like that." Lyra rolled her eyes.

They both laughed, and for the first time in weeks

Dion was able to relax. That was until his cell phone rang and he looked down at the screen.

"Problem?" Lyra asked.

"With a capital *P*" was his reply. "Excuse me a minute." He pressed the talk button and said, "Dion Donovan."

"Where the hell are you? We were supposed to meet for dinner."

There was a time—Dion fought desperately to remember—when he'd thought the deep smoky timbre of Katrina Saldana's voice was attractive. Lately, however, every time he heard her voice, the sound grated on his nerves just a little more.

"I'm having dinner now and you're interrupting," he said sternly.

"What? You're having dinner where? With whom? Okay, no, don't answer that. Just pick me up when you finish, we need to talk," she said, clearly exasperated with him again.

"Not tonight," he said in a clipped tone.

"Why not?"

"Because I said not tonight."

"Then tomorrow? Or will you stand me up then, too?"

This wasn't a conversation Dion wanted to repeat, but if she insisted on ignoring the obvious he'd tell her again. "Listen, Katrina, we've talked about all we need to talk about. I thought you understood where we stand now."

She sighed heavily. "Dion, I just want to talk to you. Really, baby, you're being petty by avoiding my calls and standing me up."

"And you're being unrealistic. I don't think there's anything else for us to talk about."

"I disagree."

"Then that's something you'll have to work out on your own." Dion disconnected the call before Katrina could respond, no doubt irritating him even more.

"Katrina the Clinger," Lyra said, putting a forkful of pork into her mouth and smiling as she chewed.

"Shut up and eat."

"I thought you said you broke up with her?" she said, covering her mouth as she chewed.

"I did. Apparently she doesn't listen very well."

"Apparently. So who are you seeing now since you've let Katrina and her gold-plated hooks go?"

"Why do you keep referring to her by some tabloid-created name?"

"Because she's exactly what the tabloids describe—an opportunistic gold digger who'll set her sights on any rich man who will put a ring on it and maintain her luxurious lifestyle."

He had to chuckle at that, since she'd managed to say it with a straight face like she was just stating the facts.

"That's exactly why I ended things with her," he said, only half truthfully.

"But everybody wants to be with Dion Donovan. Your reputation precedes you, sir."

Dion finished off his water, then reached for the cold beer he'd ordered. "Well, it's a good thing you know me better than my reputation."

Propping her elbows on the table Lyra simply watched him. "Yeah, it's a good thing."

* * *

They didn't talk about Katrina anymore, which suited Dion just fine. Instead he was able to thoroughly enjoy the time alone with Lyra—time he'd missed too much while she'd been away.

Since she was staying at the Big House, that's where Dion followed her to in his car. His intention was to see her inside, then return to his condo. But of course, where Lyra was concerned, things hardly ever went as they were supposed to.

"I still love walking around here," she said when they were once again alone on the dock. "It's so quiet. And yet just a few feet out on the water there's always a boat full of people, or someone on a jet ski, or lovers out for a midnight sail. It's peaceful and picturesque. I really missed this in L.A."

"Nothing peaceful about L.A.," he said, standing next to her. The scent of her perfume wafted on the breeze, permeating his senses and hardening his body.

"You're right." She sighed, folding her arms over her chest.

They stood in silence for a few minutes as Dion slipped his hands into his pockets. "You remember the last time we stood here?"

She didn't answer right away.

"Two nights ago when I came back" was her slow reply.

"No," he answered. "The time before that...."

Water lapped against the wooden piles of the dock, and darkness seemed to suddenly surround them.

"I remember," she said.

"I can't forget it—the way you looked, your scent, your voice." The entire scene had replayed in his mind like somebody had hit the rewind button for the last ten years.

Lyra didn't speak.

"I thought about you so much while you were away," Dion continued, not sure why he felt the sudden urge to confess his deepest feelings where she was concerned.

"I kept in touch," she whispered, then cleared her throat. "We wrote to each other and texted."

"But you weren't here," he said simply, then turned so he was now facing her. "You weren't just down the hall so that I could knock on your door and in seconds see your face. You were thousands of miles away." He took a deep breath and waited a beat until she looked up at him. "I missed you."

Chapter 7

Lyra's heart beat a frantic rhythm in her chest. He was standing so close. The sky was lit with tiny twinkling stars and the water shimmered from the glow cast by the moonlight. A more romantic setting she'd never find, and yet she was afraid.

"I missed being home, too," she said, thinking it was a safe reply.

The corner of his mouth lifted in a smile that said he knew that wasn't what she really wanted to say. Of course, Lyra realized that what she did want to say was wrong. And the thoughts running through her mind and the feeling of arousal humming through her body was also wrong. It was a betrayal of her engagement to Mark, and she knew she should have been ashamed of herself.

"I should have told you to stay," he said, knocking her further off-kilter.

"Dion," she barely whispered before his hands were reaching to cup her face.

She tried to take a step back but he held her close.

"You told me to give you a reason to stay and I didn't. I had reasons, but I didn't give you any. I was wrong," he said, looking deeply into her eyes.

Crap! she thought. Lyra should've turned and run as fast as she could into the house, to the safety of her room. She should have pushed him away, reminded him she was engaged. Instead Lyra found herself standing completely still, her hands reaching to touch his wrists.

"It's done. We've both moved on."

"Have we?" he asked sincerely. "No one else has been able to take the memory of our kiss from my mind."

"Mark" was all she could manage to say next.

"Do you love him?"

"Of course." Lyra cleared her suddenly dry throat again. "I'm marrying him?"

He raised a questioning brow and she wanted to throw herself off that dock into the chilly water. Dion could see right through her, he always had.

"It's too late for this, Dion. We had our moment and it slipped away. We both lead different lives now."

"And yet, here we are again, right back where we started."

Lyra was shaking her head as he pulled her closer.

"Kiss me, Lyra. One more time, I want you to kiss me and then tell me to go."

"You're not being fair," she whimpered.

He chuckled. "There's no such thing as fair when I want something. You know that, Lyra."

"But you can't have me. Not now," Lyra replied.

Dion only stared at her and slowly lowered his head. Her eyes were closing before her mind could warn them not to and his lips touched hers. Every muscle in her body seemed to melt and meld to his body as she tiptoed, slid her hands up his arms and across his broad shoulders, wrapping them around his neck.

His hands moved from her face, down around her waist where he held on tight. Fitting her closely to his body, he let the force of his kiss press her lips until they opened, their tongues touching with a heated flash that soared right through her body.

This was a hungry kiss, a needy exchange that seemed to go on forever and ever. The memory of that first innocent kiss that burned in her mind was replaced by the scorching reality of their still unfulfilled desire. Her heart hammered wildly and her fingers clenched his shirt before Dion slowly pulled away.

"Are you sure I can't have you, Lyra?"

Reality took hold with the sudden breeze as Lyra felt the weight of guilt pressing against her temples. She pulled her hands away from him as if he'd singed her. She took several steps backward and breathed deeply.

When she felt composed enough, she looked up at him and saw the familiar dark brown eyes, creamy skin tone and chiseled outline of his face. He was just as she'd remembered him and so much more. He was her best friend and confidant and the biggest threat to her happiness. And he was also her past.

"You had your chance, Dion. I was willing to give you everything. It's too late now."

Lyra turned and walked quickly away before he came up with some argument that would wear away her defenses. She kept going until she was in her room, had closed the door and had safely locked it behind her. Only then did she allow herself to truly breathe. Her fingers touched her still-swollen lips.

What had she just done?

Chapter 8

Long acrylic nails tapped an annoying rhythm on the marble kitchen countertop. The heel of Katrina Saldana's four-and-a-half-inch sling-back shoe clicked against the tile floor in a synchronized melody, as the air crackled with tension.

Katrina was not a happy woman.

"Bastard!" she yelled, tossing her now-empty champagne glass across the room so that it shattered into shards, scattering across the floor.

Dion Donovan was not breaking up with her, plain and simple. She'd invested almost five months in their relationship, and that wasn't including the year and a half she'd spent plotting how to get close to him. Now he wanted to act like she didn't exist, like she was just supposed to take his rejection lying down. Well, he had no idea who he was dealing with. In two years she'd be thirty. That was her deadline for being married to someone rich and famous so that she'd be set financially and socially for the rest of her life.

Dion was her carefully selected mark. With so many scrumptious Donovan men walking around, she had to set her sights on the one most likely to satisfy all her needs. He was the eldest son in Miami's Donovan family and the head of *Infinity Magazine,* which meant he was the first in line to inherit everything. His cousins were all successful and handsome as well, but Dion's laid-back personality combined with his macho self-confidence had aroused something in her from the first night she'd met him at Glimmer, a South Beach club he frequented—or used to frequent. In the past two months, she'd felt him pulling away, and the increasing distance between them was not a good thing.

About two months ago they'd had "the talk." Whatever that meant. Katrina wasn't sure, since she had never been given the brush-off by any man before. In past relationships, things were either on or off, and the decision was almost always hers. Maybe that's why the fact that Dion was avoiding her stung so much? No, it was more. She had feelings for Dion—as much as she could have feelings for any man—even though men hadn't always been particularly kind to Katrina in her twenty-eight years.

But that was all about to change. Dion was going to be hers, even if she had to use unconventional methods to make him see that.

She ignored the mess she'd made, leaving it for the maid to clean up once she thought it was safe to come out of hiding and escape being the brunt of one of Katrina's tantrums. Katrina walked out onto the balcony.

It wasn't her fault that the household staff was afraid of her. Then again, it was a good thing they were. Katrina liked telling people what to do and daring them to disobey her. Maintaining her staff was another reason she needed Dion Donovan. Her money was running low, and even though there were other men willing to help keep her from resorting to her previous occupation as an exotic dancer, she'd rather be married to a continuous cash flow than relying on tips and favors here and there.

She pulled her cell phone out of the pocket of her pleated champagne-colored slacks. Hitting speed dial, she put the phone to her ear and waited while it rang.

"Hello?" a deep voice answered.

"Hi, stranger," she replied with a less-than-genuine smile, but she tried to make her voice sound cheerful.

"Well, if it isn't my favorite lady. To what do I owe the pleasure of this call? Last I heard you were clubbing it up with that rich Donovan dude."

"That's what I'm calling you about," she said, looking out into the darkening sky. "I need your help."

"Oh? What kind of help? Something that'll necessitate my getting naked, I hope."

"Stop it." She laughed at his comment, but knew that the last thing she wanted was to sleep with him again for a favor. And knowing him, he wasn't thinking of just the two of them, either. That's just how he was. "I just need you to back me up. I've got something in the works and I need to know I can count on you for confirmation."

"Confirmation of what?" he asked.

Katrina sighed. He could be so slow at times.

"Of whatever I say."

"And what's in it for me?"

She'd known that question was coming. "What you've wanted for a long, long time."

He was silent for a few seconds then he chuckled. "If you can make that happen I'll swear you're the Queen of England."

Tapping her nail on the back of the cell phone Katrina smiled. "I'll just bet you will."

Guilt assailed Lyra the second she opened her eyes and pulled herself out of the bed. In the shower she prayed the water would wash away her deceit, even though all she'd really done was kiss Dion. She'd done that before and it had been no big deal. There was really no reason for her to think differently now. Except that the last time Dion had kissed her he'd sent her away. No, that was too dramatic. He hadn't wanted a future with her and thus told her to go to L.A.

She'd done that and she'd fallen for another man who now wanted to marry her. That should have been all that mattered—not the intensity of Dion's kiss, the warmth of his lips, or the delicious stroke of his tongue along hers.

Lyra tilted her face upward toward the steamy shower spray and prayed that the stream of water cascading down her body would somehow wash those thoughts away. She was engaged to be married and Dion was— he was, dammit—he was still in her head.

All those years in L.A. had made her believe she'd been successful in pushing thoughts of him out of her mind. But she was wrong. He was still there, and after last night's kiss she knew without a doubt his presence was stronger than ever.

There was a knock at her door the moment she entered her room after her shower. Her intention had been to get dressed and get out of the house as quickly as possible. Even though Dion no longer lived here, his family did. The last thing Lyra wanted was for any of them to figure out how she felt about Dion. Not that she would tell them, but they all had this uncanny way of knowing things without being told. If she had been inclined to believe in the supernatural, she'd think they had ESP. Instead, she decided the Donovans had a finely honed sense of intuition.

"Come in," she heard herself say, pulling the belt to her robe tighter, just in case.

"Good morning," Janean said as she quietly entered the room, smiling as though seeing Lyra was the happiest moment of her life.

"Good morning," Lyra said letting that smile coax her into a good mood. Janean Donovan had never been anything but nice to her, and Lyra owed her the world.

"I just wanted to come in and steal a moment alone with you. You've been so busy since you came back."

Always impeccably dressed, Janean wore a lavender silk sundress today with a white jacket. She crossed the room, coming to sit beside Lyra on the edge of the bed.

"I'm just trying to get acclimated at *Infinity*. I want to do a good job," Lyra told her truthfully—at least as truthfully as she could.

"Of course you'll do a good job." Janean took Lyra's hand, the left one with Mark's engagement ring. "The boys have no doubt you'll be good. That's why they hired you."

"They hired me because you and your husband told them to," Lyra said.

Janean shook her head. "Oh, no, you should know

better. We don't do that. If you're not qualified—even if you are family—you don't work for the company. It's that simple. The station and all the other companies mean everything to Bruce and Reginald. They wouldn't hire just anybody. And you know how shrewd Sean is. If he thought for one minute you weren't going to work out, he wouldn't have agreed to your coming on board."

To a certain extent, Lyra believed her. She had studied and worked with the best in L.A., and had built quite a reputation for herself. And before the offer came from *Infinity* she'd been seriously considering accepting a lucrative offer at *Vogue*. So, yes, she believed she was qualified to do the job. Now she was questioning just how smart it had been to agree to come back and work so closely with Dion.

"You're right," she said with a smile.

"So how are you settling in?"

She nodded as if to convince herself. "I'm good. Mark is busy looking for an apartment for us, so I won't be in your hair too long."

"Nonsense!" Janean waved a hand, catching the sunlight that poured in from the windows, making the diamonds in her rings sparkle. "What's gotten into you talking so silly this morning? This is your home. You can stay here as long as you like."

"I feel like the child who hasn't left the nest."

"But you did leave. You just came back. And we know it's only temporary, but Bruce and I are happy you're here just the same."

"Thanks. You've always been so nice to me."

"Now, don't patronize me. I'm going to get angry if you do, and I know you don't want that."

Lyra sobered immediately. "No, ma'am."

"Everything that Bruce and I have done for you is from our hearts. We love you, Lyra. You're our daughter no matter what."

Those words had been said so many times in the years she'd known the Donovans. She'd been welcome in their home from that first day. And she was more than grateful for that.

"What's going on with the wedding? Have you and Mark set a date yet?"

Lyra stiffened. She realized she did and hoped that Janean didn't notice it. Clearing her throat and lifting her hand to her mouth faking a cough, she tried to play it off. "We're, um, we're going to. I mean, the apartment hunting is first on the agenda."

Janean nodded, eyeing Lyra suspiciously.

"Have you and Dion been okay at work?"

Wow, what an abrupt change of subject.

"Sure."

"I saw his car here last night. Thought he'd come around and speak to me, but he never did. I figured the two of you had been together."

Together? What did that mean? "Ah, we had dinner at Shorty's. I missed their barbecue." Lyra tried to smile, but it came out as a nervous laugh.

Janean was watching her closely—too closely. "You and Dion always did hang out a lot. I'm glad he's been there for you."

"Me, too."

There was a pause and Lyra just wanted to scream. A part of her wanted to tell Janean everything, to pour out her heart to her. But she'd never poured out her heart to anyone—except Dion. Only now she couldn't tell him what she truly felt. She couldn't confide in him, because to do so would change everything.

Janean patted Lyra's hand. "Lyra, if there's anything you ever want to tell me or talk to me about, you know I'm here."

She nodded. "Yes, ma'am."

"I know you've prided yourself on being independent since you graduated from high school, but understand that I'm here for you, just like always."

Those words had Lyra relaxing slightly. "I know. And I appreciate everything you and your family have done for me. I'm just trying to get my head around the new job and finding a place and getting married. It's a lot."

Janean was still giving Lyra a funny look. "Yes it is," she said. "Life has a way of changing sometimes, and it feels like you're spinning out of control. But don't fret. There's always a plan. We may not know what it is or how it'll play out, but there's a plan for each of us."

Janean had often told her that during her childhood. Lyra only hoped the plan for her was something she could live with.

Chapter 9

"This is the second apartment you didn't like," Mark said with more than a touch of frustration.

Lyra tried not to roll her eyes. She looked out the car window instead. "It's on the top floor, twenty-two flights up. I was getting sick standing on the balcony."

"It's an exclusive condo. They just started selling units last month. It's the newest building in Miami and you're complaining about how high up it is."

There was a time when the sound of Mark's voice made her feel a certain way. Not warm and passionate, but comfortable and safe. Today it was grating on her nerves. Truth be told, she'd been annoyed since receiving the email from Vina's people that morning saying they wanted a reshoot because the proofs she sent over weren't good enough. She'd wanted to tell them it was because Vina was a little buzzed and her people were all whackos who had little control over her. Instead, she emailed them a quick response suggesting another time for the reshoot, but was clear that this would be the last photo shoot before the magazine went to press with whatever shots they decided on. She wasn't in the business of jumping through hoops for any client, no matter how many times they topped the music charts.

Mark had only called four times during the day to remind her of the appointments they had this evening to look at places. She'd wanted to hang up the last three times. But this was the man she would be sharing the rest of her life with—the one with whom she needed to find a place to live. *I'd better start getting used to the sound of his voice again,* she thought.

"I just didn't like it. Newer doesn't necessarily mean better."

"Fine," he replied. "Then where would you like to live? I mean, since I'm the only one even looking for a place."

"I just started a new job, Mark. You could give me a second to get acclimated. It's not like we're both sleeping at a hotel or on the streets. Your parents are more than happy to have you at home with them."

"And let me guess, the Donovans are more than happy to have you staying with them."

Now Lyra did sigh. This was the beginning of a ten-year-long-running argument that she and Mark always had but never quite seemed to resolve. She turned a little, and at first just looked at his profile. He was angry. That little muscle in his jaw was tensing. His mocha-toned face was capped by the thin goatee he sported. He wasn't a big man, but slim and fit in his dress slacks and shirt. The jacket and tie he'd worn to work were neatly folded on the backseat.

"We're going to find a place and it's going to be wonderful. But we don't have to do it in one afternoon. That's the point I'm trying to make."

Mark nodded. "How long do you plan to stay there?"

The interior of the car was suddenly quiet. Lyra felt sick. The question was a simple one and should have only required a simple answer. Yet she felt like there was a deeper meaning, like Mark was really asking her something else entirely. Something she was afraid to admit to herself, let alone say aloud to him.

"Until we find a place," she said hesitantly.

"Mmm-hmm." He frowned and turned into the driveway of his parents' home.

"I thought we were going to dinner," Lyra said, her heart starting to pound. She didn't want to see his parents. They would no doubt ask about the wedding plans and their living arrangements and all the things you usually asked an engaged couple. His mother would want to know if they'd set a date and how soon they planned on starting a family, all of which were things Mark had wanted to discuss, as well. All of which felt like a black cloud hanging over Lyra's head.

"I wanted some alone time with you. Is that all right?" he asked, bringing the car to a stop that jolted her.

Lyra licked her lips and tried to smile. "That's fine," she whispered before he unlocked the doors.

She didn't wait for him to come around and open her door but stepped out of the car on her own. When he kept walking to the door Lyra felt like she had to do something. This was all her fault, the tension between them. It was her connection to the Donovans, her link to Dion that was making Mark crazy. She knew that, had always known that he suspected something was going on between the two of them. But he was wrong, there was nothing there, they were just best friends.

Catching up with him she touched his arm. "You're right," she said when he turned to look at her. "Finding a place of our own and starting our lives together should be my first priority. I apologize if I haven't been acting like it."

His jaw slackened, his eyes softened. He touched a hand to her cheek. "I just want you to be my wife and for us to be happy. That's all."

She nodded. "I know."

He slipped the key into the door and pushed it open. Touching the small of her back he led her inside and Lyra decided then and there that Dion's kisses, his touches, any dreams she'd had of them being any more than friends had to end tonight. Mark was her future. Dion was a dream from the past.

"Hello?"

She sounded groggy. He'd awakened her. A part of him was glad she was in bed asleep at one in the morning. Another part wondered if she was alone in that bed.

"Hey. Dreaming of me?"

She sighed and it sounded like she shifted the phone or was moving around herself. "I was dreaming, period. That means I'm supposed to be asleep and not on the phone" was Lyra's reply.

Dion laughed. It was the same reply she'd given him anytime he'd called her at night, something he used to do quite often when she was away at college. It seemed that was the time he did his best thinking. And usually that thinking involved Lyra.

"So how was your day?" he asked settling down in the leather recliner across from his bed.

"It was a day. How was yours?"

It really didn't matter that she was sleeping. Just like it didn't matter what he was doing whenever she needed him. It was like that between them. They were always there for each other no matter what. He wondered if that would change when she married what's-his-name.

"Long. Meetings at the office all afternoon. Then a dinner meeting that ended with cocktails."

"More about the expansion?"

"Yeah, we're moving ahead pretty quickly, trying to stay one step ahead of the competition."

"That's a good plan, but you don't want to move so fast you make a mistake. Is Sean doing all the research?"

Dion rubbed a hand down the back of his head and massaged the back of his neck. He desperately needed the real thing but hadn't had the time lately. "Sean and his team, they've done a great job. It's the implementation we're working on. Savian's already managing the network, but adding new programming has to go through the entire board."

"Right. Are you just presenting the reality show for Camille?"

"No. I did talk to Adam today. He and Camille are thinking of coming out for the ball so we can talk a little more about the show. But Regan's presenting the fashion segment. Parker's thinking about adding her to DNT's nightly entertainment show for a trial run. There's a lot going on."

Lyra huffed. "Tell me about it."

By this time Dion concluded she was alone. No way would she be able to continue talking to him if her man was in bed beside her. He was elated at that realization.

"You having problems at work?" he asked with concern.

"No. Not work. Well, Vina's being a bitch, but I expected that."

"That goes with the territory for her. You don't have to do the reshoot."

"How did you know about that?"

"I see all the editorial revisions at the end of the day. I saw the proofs, too, and we could just as easily go with one of them."

"And have her get pissed off on my first shoot? No, thank you. I'll do the reshoot, but I told her people this is their last chance. She needs to sober up and take the damned picture."

"That's a girl. You've still got that spunk. Now tell me what else is going on?"

"Nothing," she said after a few seconds of silence.

"Come on, Lyra, we've never kept secrets from each other. Something's bothering you. Tell me. Maybe I can help."

"You can't fix everything, Dion. I know you're an almighty Donovan and all, but you cannot fix everything."

Her voice had changed when she said that and it almost seemed like she was repeating something someone else had said.

"Whoa, wait a minute. What does that mean?"

"I'm sorry." He heard her take a deep breath, then let it out slowly. She'd probably closed her eyes and silently counted to ten before speaking again. That's how she kept her feelings under control.

"I didn't mean it to come out that way. I just meant that there are some things I have to do for myself."

"Okay. I agree. Some battles are yours to fight. But you're my best friend, Lyra. If there's something going on with you, I'm not about to just sit by and let you drive yourself crazy trying to figure it out. Just tell me what's going on."

Again she was quiet, and for a minute he thought she was actually going to keep this to herself. There was something different about her since she'd come back from L.A. It was barely noticeable, but Dion could see it. She'd changed in a way he wasn't quite sure how to handle.

"I'm just...a little nervous, I guess," she finally admitted.

"Nervous about what?"

"Change."

He'd figured as much. In the weeks before she'd left for L.A., Lyra had been moody and cranky and almost unbearable to be around. He knew it was because she was leaving and that it would be the first time she was on her own. Still, Dion had sensed a sort of urgency in her during that time. She wanted to leave Miami, wanted to prove to herself that she could make it on her own, finally. And he'd supported that. So when she asked him to give her a reason to stay he had plenty, the first one being him. He'd wanted her to stay to be with him. Instead, he'd given her what he knew she needed— even though at the time she didn't want to hear it.

"Life is about change, Lyra. We all have to adjust to

it on some level. At least you're back home now with your family to support you."

"Right," she said with another sigh. "Mark wants to hurry up. He wants us to set the wedding date."

Dion's gut clenched. He didn't want her to marry Mark. Hell, he hadn't liked the idea of Mark heading to L.A. with her all those years ago, either. And for a man used to getting what he wanted, holding back where Lyra was concerned was becoming harder and harder for him. The fact was Lyra was different. She wasn't like any of the other women Dion had wanted, mainly on a temporary basis. This need for her had rooted itself in him years ago. It was around the time she turned sixteen and he saw her in a way that wasn't sisterly. They'd already cemented their friendship and it had blossomed into something more. Yet he'd kept in mind how important she was to his parents, how tumultuous her upbringing had been and how if he wasn't totally serious about committing to her, it might mess up the best friendship he'd ever had. And so he'd backed off.

Dion wasn't sure he could do that now.

"If you don't want to marry him then don't," he replied simply.

"It's not that. I don't think. I just don't see the reason for rushing."

"How much more time do you need to think about it?" he asked, wondering if she really loved this guy.

"That's just it. I don't know."

"Then let me ask you this. Do you love him?"

She was quiet and Dion had his answer. If he could've sung he would have. Instead he smiled to himself, rubbing a finger over his chin. Lyra wasn't in love with Mark. And she'd kissed him the other night with a desire so intense he'd dreamed of her all night long. In his mind that meant one thing—it was time to make his move.

"I should love him. He's been great to me over the years. He's a good man with a good future. Everything a girl like me ever dreamed of."

"A girl like you?"

"You know what I mean, Dion. I've never expected too much. I couldn't afford to. With Mark I didn't really have to. He was just there and he did all the right things, made all the right moves. We should be married."

"Even if you don't love him?"

"I didn't say I didn't love him."

"You didn't say you did, either."

She made this mumbling sound and then it sounded like she moved around again. *She was probably sitting up in the bed now, ready to debate him,* he thought.

"All I'm saying is on paper everything looks perfect. We seem to make a good couple. I just want to be absolutely sure that it's right in every other respect before I make such a huge commitment."

She was trying to convince herself to settle is what it sounded like to Dion. She deserved better. After all she'd been through, Lyra deserved to have real love, real passion and Dion knew he was the man who could give that to her.

"What about us, Lyra?"

"What about us?" she asked hesitantly.

"There's something going on between us. You know that. You knew it before you left for L.A. and you know it now."

What Lyra knew was that she shouldn't have answered the phone. She'd looked at the display on her cell and saw it was Dion. A part of her smiled, and remembered all their late-night conversations when she'd been away at college and wanted to feel that nostalgia again. Another part felt guilty, a feeling that was beginning to make itself right at home with her lately.

"We knew the boundaries before and we honored them. Now that I'm back, we just have to remember them."

"You know me better than that. I don't work with boundaries."

"I know. You're a Donovan, so you do what you want and you get what you want. You don't have to remind me of that, Dion. But if I remember correctly, you're the one who sent me away. When I was ready to explore what was happening between us, you told me to go." *And broke every piece of my heart,* she thought.

"There was a reason for that."

"It doesn't matter. It was the right thing to do. Just like we both know now that the right thing to do is to remain friends."

"Why? Because on paper it looks like Mark is the right man for you?"

"Mark and I are better suited for each other, that's all. He's more my type."

"What? How can you say that and know that you're trying to figure out if you love him enough to marry him?"

"We just make a better couple. With Mark I don't feel like I'm reaching, trying to be a part of something I'm not." The words were out of her mouth before Lyra could stop them. On the other end of the phone Dion was quiet and she knew that wasn't a good thing.

"Are you talking about our backgrounds, Lyra? Are

you really going to bring up the fact that you come from a different background than I do? We grew up in the same house, dammit!"

"But only one of us belonged here," she admitted, looking around the bedroom that she was still amazed to call her own. It was an ugly truth, one that probably hurt Dion as much as it hurt her to admit. He was from a different class. If not for Dion's mother and her generous heart, they most likely would have never met. They wouldn't have gone to the same schools or even gone to the same places. He would have remained in his social circle and she would have remained in hers. At least Mark had come from a simple working-class family. His rise to wealth had been the result of a lot of financial aid and some luck thrown in. Just like Lyra had lucked out.

"That's ridiculous and you know it. Did Mark tell you that? Is that what he feeds you to keep you with him?"

"He doesn't have to feed me lines, Dion. He's not the billionaire playboy like you. He's not the one with his picture in the tabloids and stories of his sexual exploits. He's a simple guy and I'm a simple woman. That's a good match."

"That's bullshit!"

The line went silent again and Lyra took a deep steadying breath.

"I don't want to lose you as a friend, Dion. Your family means a lot to me. But this is my life and I have to make the choices that are best for me."

She waited a minute, not sure what she wanted to hear from him at this moment but shocked that she heard absolutely nothing.

"I thought you, of all people, would understand," she added and then because the silence hurt almost as much as the day he'd told her to leave, Lyra disconnected the call.

Chapter 10

Dion was in a crappy mood.

That was probably an understatement. But his staff knew when to steer clear of him. He hadn't taken any calls all morning and had barely read a word of the latest sales figures and projections that were on his desk when he came in. All he could think about was Lyra.

Of all the things standing between them he'd never expected it to be something as meaningless as money.

Lyra had come to live with them when she was ten years old. Dion was fourteen and Sean was eleven. Neither one of them particularly cared for girls at the time, but their mother had been adamant about them being nice to Lyra because she'd had a hard life. At the time Dion didn't have a clue what that meant, but out of respect for his mother he gave Lyra a break.

Right from the start she'd been a fighter, giving as

good as she got, whenever he and Sean had plotted against her. In most cases she bested them. So it wasn't long before the brothers had accepted her as their little sister—not only in their home, but in their hearts. On the playground they defended her—even though most times they really didn't need to. Lyra had a way of taking care of herself. She wasn't always as forthright as Dion would have liked, but she always handled things in her own way. He wondered why he had such a hard time believing she'd do the same now.

Because there was a man involved, a man who had been intimately involved in her life for the past ten years, while Dion had been hundreds of miles away sleeping with women whose names he could barely remember.

Speaking of which, Katrina had called the office four times for him already. He'd switched his cell phone to silent because she continuously called it, as well. He'd told her it was over and didn't really know what else to say to her. But it was clear she wasn't taking that very well. It had been years since he'd had a messy breakup, and he really didn't feel like going through one now. What he wanted was time to deal with Lyra. He wanted to spend time with her, to make her see that they could be perfect on paper just as she thought she and Mark were. It sounded juvenile, but Dion didn't give a damn. He knew what he wanted and he wasn't about to let her walk out of his life again.

The knock on his door only made him frown even more. He'd told everyone he didn't want to be disturbed. Apparently, someone hadn't listened. With a huff he stood and walked over to the door, ready to deliver some choice words to whoever was bold enough to bother him. When he opened the door, staring back at him was Mark Stanford. Dion paused momentarily. "Come in."

Mark walked past him and Dion closed the door behind him. He had no idea what this visit was about. Then again, he did. Even though he didn't think the man was right for Lyra, Dion had to respect Stanford as an intelligent brother on the come up. He'd worked at Zuratech as a program manager in L.A. and just recently had taken over as CEO of LinearSearch, a growing search engine that was reportedly going to take the internet by storm.

He was an inch or two shorter than Dion, about fifty or so pounds lighter, but was impeccably dressed in a suit, tie and well-shined dress shoes. Mark took a seat in one of the guest chairs while Dion moved around his desk to sit in his own chair.

"How's it going, Mark?" he asked in a voice as calm and controlled as he could muster.

"Well," said Mark, in an even more controlled reply, "I want to talk to you about Lyra."

Mark had thrown down the gauntlet, so to speak. He was here for a reason, probably to stake his claim and to tell Dion to back off. He'd come in person instead of sending a message via Lyra or calling on the phone. Dion had to respect the man's gumption. Even if this was a battle *he* fully expected to win.

"It's great to have her back home and working for the family where she belongs," he said, knowing Mark didn't care for either situation. To make matters worse, Dion added a smile and had the pleasure of watching Mark's eyes grow darker.

"We're getting married. She'll be moving out of your parents' home soon. I just wanted you to understand that our goal is to start our own family as soon as possible. I know she values her job here and I don't want to interfere with that. But I don't want her overworked, either."

Wow, Dion thought. Mark continued to surprise him.

"I can assure you that I have Lyra's best interests in mind at all times. She'll be fine."

"She's already stressed, trying to do a good job to impress you and your family. She feels like she owes you people something and it's wearing her down. I want that to stop."

Did he just say *you people?* Dion's smile quickly turned into the frown he'd had just moments before Mark had interrupted.

"We're Lyra's family, don't forget that. I understand that you're engaged to her. But we've known her a lot longer than you have. I think we know what's best for her."

"Your family's taking advantage of her," Mark accused. "And especially you."

Slowly, Dion leaned forward letting his elbows rest on his desk and twining his fingers together to try to resist the urge to reach out and punch Mark in the face.

"Let's cut to the chase here, Mark. You're threatened by my relationship with Lyra. Correct?"

Mark didn't appear the least bit fazed by Dion's cool tone. He looked him directly in the eye. "I don't like your relationship with Lyra. You manipulate her every chance you get, and I'm here to tell you I've had enough."

"Lyra is very important to me. There's nothing I wouldn't do for her, and I don't plan to change that in any way."

"I'm asking you man to man to stand down. She's not your responsibility anymore. She's mine."

The last was said with a smirk that really made Dion's fingers itch. He hadn't punched anyone in years, but he would come out of hibernation for Mark Stanford. Then again, physical violence wasn't necessary. They were both men, who just happened to want the same woman. At the end of the day, the choice would be Lyra's. And no matter what, Dion promised himself he'd respect her final decision. But he'd never walked away from a challenge in his life, and today wasn't going to be any different.

"If she's yours you have nothing to worry about," he said smiling once more. "Now is that all you wanted to say?"

Mark stood. Dion followed suit.

"Leave her alone," Mark said, adjusting his suit jacket and buttoning it. "Or you'll be sorry."

"Don't come in my office and threaten me, Mark. You have no idea what I'm capable of."

"Likewise," Mark said, before turning and walking to the door. He let himself out quietly but didn't have a chance to close the door as Sean and Parker were apparently on their way to see him. After his brother and cousin walked in, Dion sat down heavily in his chair.

"Why do I have the feeling we just interrupted something?" Parker said, his usual grin replaced by a more concerned look.

"Wasn't that Mark Stanford?" Sean asked closing the door. "Lyra's fiancé?"

Dion nodded. "The one and only."

"What did he want? I'm sure it wasn't to ask you to

be the best man at his wedding," Parker said, lamely attempting a joke.

Dion faced both of them and said with a lightness that baffled him. "To stake his claim on Lyra, and to tell me to back the hell off."

"Was that necessary?" Parker asked.

Sean eyed Dion, then sighed. "Yeah, I think it was."

"It wasn't necessary because I'm not intimidated by him" was Dion's calm reply. "I can't help it if the man's insecure."

Parker chuckled.

"Is there a need for his insecurity?" Sean asked.

"Come on, we're talking about Lyra. She's family," Parker interjected.

But Sean held Dion's gaze, giving him a knowing look without saying a word.

With a nod Dion conceded, "It might be."

"What?"

"Jeez!"

Sean and Parker's responses came simultaneously.

"Are you kidding? You're messing with little Lyra?"

"Parker," Sean said. "She's a grown woman."

"She's the little twerp we've been teasing forever" was Parker's reply.

"What she is," Dion said, "is old enough to make her own decisions. If she doesn't want Stanford, then she doesn't have to marry him."

"And if she wants you?" Sean asked.

Dion shrugged. "It is what it is."

Sean was shaking his head. "Don't mess with her, man. Mom will kill you if you break her heart."

"Why does everyone think the worst of me when

it comes to women? I'm not always out to break their hearts," Dion implored.

Sean and Parker looked at each other, then back at Dion.

"You're not?" Parker said with a grin. "You're in the headlines every six weeks or so for doing precisely that. Come to think of it," he said, tossing a tabloid onto Dion's desk. "Take a look at yesterday's headline."

WEDDING BELLS FOR PLAYBOY DONOVAN?

The headline was big and bold over a picture of Dion and Katrina leaving a nightclub.

"This is bull!" Dion said, pushing the paper away.

"But it proves our point," Sean replied. "Lyra is not to be played with, Dion. You wouldn't sit by and let any other man mess with her emotions. I'm not going to sit by and watch you do it."

"What if I'm not messing with her emotions? What if this is real for me?" Dion asked, for the millionth time in weeks believing in his heart that what he felt for Lyra was real. More real then he'd ever thought he'd feel for any woman.

"Then Stanford's fighting a losing battle. He's no match for a Donovan," Parker said, his expression now seemingly serious.

Chapter 11

When Lyra got the call she wanted to scream. It was one hell of a homecoming, but she shouldn't have expected anything less. Outside of being an addict, her mother was a total drama queen. Her mother's call crying and babbling about being hurt and feeling like she was dying was probably a hangover from some drug or drinking binge. Even after almost twenty years of filling her body with toxins, it wasn't too far-fetched that her mother would be feeling something close to death.

It was that thought that made Lyra jump out of bed, slip on sweatpants and a T-shirt and head to her car. Now she was driving the streets of south Miami, beyond the glitz and glamour of South Beach and the nightlife. Her windows were rolled down and cool air slapped against her face, almost freezing the tears that wouldn't stop flowing. She was so sick of this. It was like a horrible memory all coming back. Her mother was in trouble again, and she—the child—was rushing to help her. It wasn't supposed to be this way. She wasn't supposed to be the one picking up the pieces all the time.

And yet here she was.

Turning into the driveway of some dilapidated house, Lyra cut the engine and wiped at her eyes, taking deep breaths over and over again. She couldn't count, her mind was too clouded, her thoughts too furious. Instead she snatched the keys out of the ignition and got out of the car. Heading to the house, she went straight to the back door and into the darkness.

No, she'd never been here before, just decided to follow the sounds she heard once she was inside. It was a low, moaning sound, and when she finally entered in to another room and stepped over whatever was lying on the floor she found her mother curled in a fetal position just beneath the window. The glare from a street light illuminated her form, and Lyra fell to her knees beside her.

"Mama? Mama?" she called to her. "I'm here. It's Lyra."

Paula's response was a high-pitched wail as she turned over onto her back. Lyra noted the clothes her mother wore were too small—a halter top that barely covered her small breasts and skintight pants that were now sliding down her narrow hips.

"It hurts, baby," Paula wailed.

"Yeah. I bet it does," Lyra replied grimly. Slipping her arms beneath Paula's, she lifted her mother until her wobbly legs held her in an upright position. "Let's get you out of here."

"I wanna go home, baby. You remember home?" Paula said, her head rolling onto Lyra's shoulder as she tried to walk.

"I remember, Mama." Lyra did remember, although she didn't want to. She remembered the one-bedroom apartment she and Paula shared and the great dinners they'd have around the first of the month before all the money ran out. She remembered watching the small black-and-white television while Paula sat at the table with the one wobbly chair and the other one that only had three legs so they had to prop it up with cinderblocks. Paula would be working out formulas to play her numbers—she swore they'd be rich someday. Look at them now.

They were at the door when Paula bent over, yelling in pain. Her fingers clenched Lyra's arm until Lyra wanted to scream right along with her. "Okay," Lyra said when the pain in her arm subsided only slightly. "We should get you to a hospital."

"Nooooo, I wanna go home," Paula cried.

"In a little bit. Let's get you feeling better first."

Fastening her mother into the front seat, Lyra pressed the backs of her hands to her eyes. She would not cry again. She would not stand here in the dark of night and cry over the pitiful state her mother was in. It wasn't her fault. It was Paula's choice. Lyra wasn't a child anymore, she shouldn't still carry this type of guilt, this pressure to take care of the woman who should have been taking care of her. This was not how life was supposed to be.

But it was what it was. And Lyra had always known that.

Slipping into the driver's side seat a little more composed, she drove her mother to the hospital emergency room and checked her in.

Three hours later, Paula was sleeping quietly and being treated for an apparent overdose. The toxicology report still hadn't come back by the time Lyra needed to leave the hospital to go to sleep before work the next morning. Her mind was whirling with memories and regrets and anger, so much so that the idea of going back home and crawling into her bed held less and less appeal. Instead, she found herself pulling up in front of the Marquis, one of Miami's newest condo developments, and pressing the code at the gated entrance to ring Dion.

"Hello?" He sounded groggy, most likely asleep, since it was after two in the morning.

"Hi. It's me." Lyra hesitated a moment. "Can I come up?"

Her answer was a buzzing sound that opened the gates. She drove inside and parked in the rear of the garage, which was designated for visitors. There was a back door that she had to be buzzed into before she could head to the front desk and tell them of her destination. From there, Lyra headed directly to the elevators. Just before she could step into the elevator, Lyra heard a clicking sound, but when she turned there was nobody there. With a shrug she boarded and pressed the button that would take her to the ground floor. From there she'd have to go around the corner to the elevators that would take her to the tower suites where Dion lived.

He was standing at the door the moment she stepped off the elevator. Lyra paused, swallowed hard and tried to remember why she'd come here in the first place.

No man should look this good at this ungodly hour. But Dion did. He'd pulled on basketball shorts that hung a little low on his waist. She knew he'd just put them on because he slept in the nude. Years ago when he'd first revealed that fact Lyra hadn't been turned on. Now, her nipples ached at the simple knowledge.

His eyes were a little red because he'd been asleep. But his chest was perfectly chiseled, his abs so sculpted he could have been on the cover of a fitness magazine. Eventually she took a step into the hallway because the elevator doors were about to close her back in. Still, she was swallowing and trying like hell not to be attracted to this man. She didn't need lust or imaginary emotions getting in the way. She needed her friend.

Dion moved to the side, letting her walk past him into the condo while he closed and locked the door quietly behind her.

The pale gray drapes covering the floor-to-ceiling windows were drawn tightly, and her shoes made a muffled sound walking across the hardwood floors. There was a sofa, a love seat and two accent chairs, all in the same contemporary design, all black. In the center of the floor were two leather-covered cube cocktail tables covered with proofs from *Infinity Magazine,* no doubt.

Running her fingers through her hair, Lyra sat on the sofa and lay back against the pillows, which were surprisingly soft.

"What happened?"

She heard his voice but hadn't heard his approach. Her eyes were closed, and to tell the honest truth, she was afraid to open them. Her body felt like it was on fire, every inch of her was burning. She wanted to touch him, to be near him, to kiss him. It was ridiculous, and it was making her edgier than she already was.

"My mother."

His sigh was loud, which prompted Lyra to quickly open her eyes. "Please, don't start it," she said, as she looked over at him. "I can't take it tonight, Dion."

He looked at her long and hard, like he was trying to decipher her mood before proceeding. Finally he nodded and asked, "What did Paula do this time?"

"She almost died," Lyra replied.

"What?"

It was her turn to sigh as she pulled herself up letting her elbows rest on her knees. "She called me. I went to the address she gave me and found her balled up in the fetal position on the floor. I took her to the hospital and they pumped her stomach. There was some type of toxic-laced drug in her system. They haven't identified it yet, but they're sure she was poisoned."

"They're sure it isn't drugs?" Dion asked, as a split second of anger slid across Lyra's face.

"All they said so far is alcohol."

"So where is she now?"

"At Cedars. They're keeping her for observation, then she's being admitted to rehab. And before you say it," she said, holding up a hand to ward off his words because she knew exactly what they were going to be. "She promised she'd see it through this time."

"She's made that promise before."

"I know that, Dion. I don't need you to remind me."

"Okay. Okay. Just relax," he said, sliding closer and putting his hands on her shoulders. The minute he started to rub Lyra wanted to moan. She wanted to lean against him and just melt into the magnificence of his fingers.

"She didn't die. She's going to be fine."

Lyra nodded. Tears stung the backs of her eyes but

refused to fall. She'd cried for Paula so much in her lifetime she didn't know if she had any tears left for the woman.

"Why do you keep getting so worked up over her?" Dion asked quietly, his fingers still blessedly doing a great job of relaxing her.

"She's my mother" was her simple reply. "What else can I do?"

He didn't respond.

"I know she hasn't been the best mother. Hell, she might actually qualify for an award for being the worst. But she is who she is. She's never tried to be anything else. On some level I think I have to accept that. You know what I mean?"

"I understand what you're saying," he said. "But you also have to be realistic. She may never get clean. She may never be any better to you than she has been. What are you going to do if that's true?"

Lyra shrugged. "She'll still be my mother."

He leaned down and kissed her temple. "You're a good kid, Lyra."

She laughed at the way he'd said it, and his choice of words. His tone had been light, almost teasing, and that was so she would relax even more. He knew how uptight and angry her mother could make her, knew how hard she struggled with the guilt and the pain. And he knew exactly what to do and say to her to make it better. That's why she'd come here to him.

"Sometimes I wonder if I'd been different. Maybe if she hadn't had me her life would have been different."

"Having you was the best thing Paula ever did. I believe you're the reason she's still alive, Lyra. She's been sick for a very long time, but she always turns up wherever you are. You are her life, even though it seems like the drugs are."

All Lyra had ever wanted to be was important to her mother. She'd wanted to be a big enough part of her life that she'd walk away from the drugs and her street life to be with her. But that hadn't happened. So Lyra was left to struggle with feeling unwanted and alone. Well, not alone. She'd had the Donovans.

"You're so lucky. You have a great family. A great job. Your life is perfect."

"I beg to differ," Dion said with another chuckle. His hands moved to the nape of her neck and kneaded.

Lyra moaned and let her head loll back.

"Your parents are wonderful."

"My mother can be overbearing and my dad's the toughest boss you'd ever imagine."

"You have all the money you ever need. And then some."

"And that makes me a magnet for gold diggers and scammers across the nation."

"All the women want you."

"All of them except the one I want."

Lyra froze. Suddenly the good feeling of the massage had changed.

"You can have any woman in the world," she said, but wasn't really sure why. Maybe she wanted him to clarify his statement. No. She didn't. Maybe she just wanted… Lyra didn't know what the hell she wanted at this moment. The room was just too damned hot.

One hand left the nape of her neck, sliding around to whisper over her collarbone, upward to trace the line of her jaw.

"The woman I want doesn't want me."

"Oh" was her only reply after swallowing again.

She sat up, attempting to move out of his grasp, but he wasn't letting that happen. He buried his other hand in her hair, turning her head so she could face him.

"I want you, Lyra."

Oh, God, this was such a huge mistake. She shouldn't have come here, shouldn't have sat on his couch and poured her heart out to him. No, what she really shouldn't have done was let him touch her. Dammit, she didn't want him to stop touching her.

"Dion," she whispered.

"Shhh," he said, moving closer until his lips were just a breath away from hers. "Tell me you want me, Lyra. Just this once, I need to hear you say it."

Instead she said his name again. He shook his head.

"Tell me you want me."

Lyra closed her eyes tried to visualize Mark's face, but drew a blank. She tried to pull up a shred of guilt for being here with another man. That failed, too. Clenching her fists at her sides she begged for something, anything to save her. But all she was faced with was the truth.

Opening her eyes she looked into Dion's, so familiar, so honest. Denial would not come. She licked her lips and prayed this wouldn't be the beginning of the end for them.

"I want you, Dion."

Chapter 12

Dion had a favorite song. A favorite poem. Hell, he had a favorite ring tone on his phone. But none of them compared to the sound of Lyra's voice saying she wanted him. For the rest of his life those words, that tone, would be emblazoned on his memory. His chest heaved as it seemed like he'd waited forever to hear her admit she wanted him.

Right now, however, his lips were on hers, his tongue stroking sensually over hers, his body humming with the anticipation of pleasure. On their own direction Dion's hands moved down her shoulders and back up again.

He'd wanted her, wanted this moment for so long. All his reservations from years ago were washed away. It didn't matter that she'd grown up as his sister. The fact was, she wasn't his sister. She was a vital woman, with beautiful eyes and a fighting spirit. She was an excellent photographer and a loyal friend. What Lyra was, to Dion, was everything he'd ever imagined finding in a real woman.

All the glitz and glamour of the women he met meant nothing compared to her.

She kissed him with the same hunger, as if she'd been dreaming of this moment, as well. Tearing his mouth away from hers, Dion hated to end their contact but needed to hear that they were in the same place, had been for some time.

"I've wanted you for so long, Lyra," he whispered into her ear.

Her response was a deep sigh as she pressed her lithe body closer to his. "I know. I've wanted the same thing."

His fingers gripped her harder, his lips finding hers again, taking her mouth in a ferocious sweep of tongues. Pressing her back into the chair, Dion didn't hesitate to slide on top of her. He couldn't go slow, as much as he wanted to, thought he should, he just couldn't.

"Wait," she said when he'd lifted one of her legs, tucking it around him so that he was cradled between her thighs.

Through the fog of desire Dion heard her probably the second or third time she spoke and her small hands pressed against his chest. Pulling back he looked down at her. "Sorry, am I hurting you?"

She shook her head. "I think we should talk about this first. I mean, there's Mark. And…and whoever you're seeing this month. We need to think about them."

Another thing about Lyra, she was practical and conscientious, sometimes to a fault. This time, however, Dion thought as he shifted off her, she was right.

When he was sitting up next to her, he took her hand in his. "When I wrote to you that I broke things off with Katrina, that was two months ago. I haven't been with another woman since."

She looked surprised.

"You know I wouldn't lie to you, Lyra."

"I know," she said with a tentative smile. "Even though Mark and I are now engaged, I haven't slept with him in months."

"Months?" he questioned.

"Six and a half to be exact. To tell the truth I think that may have been why he finally popped the question." Now she chuckled nervously. "Maybe he thought I'd give him some if he did."

"And you didn't?" Dion was much more sober about this than she seemed to be. He suspected because her admission was saying something about her relationship with the man she planned to marry.

"No. I didn't."

"Why?"

"I couldn't" was all she said, and Dion figured it was better not to push this issue right now. Still, there was something he had to know.

"Are you going to marry him, Lyra?"

"Honestly?"

"We've never been any other way with each other."

"I just don't know. Ask me if I love him, if I'm in love with him. The answer is no. Ask me if I can see myself with him forever. No again. So you'd think the question of if I'm going to marry him or not would be simple."

Dion touched his fingers to her chin, turned her to

face him. "I think you know the answer, you're just too nice to hurt his feelings."

"I've never wanted anyone the way I've wanted you," she admitted looking him directly in the eye.

"Me, either," he added and in that moment nothing or no one else mattered. It was as it should be, him and Lyra, finally.

The walk to Dion's bedroom seemed long but Lyra knew it had only taken a few seconds. He'd switched off the lights in the living room and hallway as they went and headed straight for his nightstand to touch the lamp there until a dim golden light illuminated his king-size bed.

Lyra gasped the moment the light illuminated the room and her gaze rested on the frame beside the lamp. She walked slowly to the nightstand and picked up the picture. "I can't believe you kept this," she said, emotion clogging her throat.

"It was a one-in-a-million shot," he said, standing close to her and wrapping an arm around her shoulders. "That's what you said when you snapped the picture."

Lyra could only nod. She'd been thirteen and Dion had just turned seventeen. The Donovans were having one of their huge summer barbecues, which included the Las Vegas, Houston and Detroit branches of the family. There were easily two hundred people at the Big House and Lyra had loved the feel of family celebration the entire weekend. She'd had a moment with Dion since Regan and a couple of her cousins were off somewhere looking at fashion magazines. They'd walked along the dock, which seemed to be their favorite spot, and out of nowhere a dragonfly had appeared.

It was beautiful with its dark pink body and wings that almost seemed to glisten. It sat right on the edge of the dock and appeared to look up at them. The camera Mr. Bruce had given her for her twelfth birthday that was always around her neck was lifted instantly and the moment captured. Now she could see it had been captured for all time.

"That was a beautiful day," she said, her fingers still moving over the photo.

"It was the day I realized you weren't my sister after all."

"What?" she asked putting the frame down and turning to him. "You and Sean treated me like the hated little sister for years, even after that."

Dion was shaking his head. "But I knew you weren't. You, uh, changed a lot that year."

Lyra blushed. "I grew breasts and got my period."

He frowned at that. "Like I said, you changed. And I started to feel different around you."

"I was just a kid and you were thinking of robbing the cradle."

Dion laughed. "I know. It was all kinds of weird, and I hated myself for it every night when I went to bed. But as time went on you kept changing and I kept feeling, until you were in my every dream. I kept the picture because it was a part of you. So even though you were miles away, you were still here, with me where you belonged."

His hands cupped her face and Lyra leaned into his embrace lifting her face in anticipation of his kiss. It came with a soft sweep of lust that pooled in her lower abdomen. Then she was on tiptoe, seeking more, loving the feel of his big strong hands on her back, her bottom, lifting her to him.

"I've dreamed of watching you undress," he said his voice as husky and deep as she remembered in her own dreams.

"Then I guess I'll make your dreams come true," she said with a smile and a spurt of courage she'd never felt before in the bedroom.

No, she wasn't a virgin, but her time in bed with men—actually, only Mark—hadn't consisted of dim golden light, heated touches or the longing looks Dion was now giving her. He made her feel sexy and desirable, whereas Mark had only made her feel like the woman in the grand scheme of sex.

"Just one second," he said, turning back to his nightstand where he reached inside a drawer to pull out a wrapped condom.

Her heart gave a little stutter at the reality that she and Dion were actually about to make love. She'd waited so long for this moment. The second his eyes were once again on her she reached for the hem of her T-shirt, pulling it over her head slowly. Her outfit of sweats and a shirt wasn't terribly sexy, so she figured she'd have to add a little to the striptease.

Reaching behind her back she unlatched her bra and had the pleasure of watching Dion's eyes darken as she shifted her shoulders and let it fall to the bed. He moved closer to the bed, his arousal apparent through the baggy shorts he wore. Her nipples puckered and stung beneath his in-depth perusal.

He removed her shoes and socks, then Lyra pushed her sweatpants down her legs and off. Wearing only her bikini underwear she came to her knees on the bed and held her arms out for him.

Dion stepped out of his shorts and Lyra gulped audibly. His body was even more sculpted than she'd witnessed through his clothes. And he was endowed, very heavily so. She couldn't stop staring at him in all his glory, and her heart beat wildly in anticipation.

He put his knee on the bed, and when he was directly in front of her wrapped his arms around her waist and pulled her close. His lips covered hers in a wild kiss that ended with them both falling onto the bed, Dion ripping her underwear off. He handed her the condom and she quickly unwrapped it and sheathed him.

"You are a beautiful woman," he said, his body hovering over hers.

Lyra lifted a hand to his cheek. "You are a beautiful man."

He gave her a lopsided grin. "Men aren't beautiful."

"You are," she said decidedly, letting her hand slide down to his chest and his abs.

When her fingers gripped his length Dion sucked in a breath. She stroked him from the base to the hilt, watching the intense play of emotions on his face as his heat filled her hands. A muscle ticked in his jaw when she rubbed a finger over his tip. She licked her lips simultaneously and he groaned.

"I can play the touching game, too," he said, sliding a hand over her hip and to the inside of her thigh.

A part of Lyra wanted to beg him to touch her. But she didn't have to. His fingers lightly pressed beyond her folds, finding her center ready and wet. She sighed into the touch, wrapping her fingers even more securely around his length. When he thrust a finger inside her she bucked and called his name as pleasure rippled through her in mighty waves.

"God, I love to hear you say my name," he groaned, pulling his fingers from her center and settling his thighs between hers.

In desperate need for more, Lyra guided his length to her entrance lifting her hips to meet him.

"I'm ready, too," he said against her ear and pressed into her.

"So long," she whispered feeling him fill her in slow increments. She wanted to work her hips, to thrust against him, the pleasure was so intense. But so was his size compared to her build, and another part of her insisted she sit still, take his movements as slowly as she could.

"It seems like we've waited forever," he was saying, pulling out of her, then thrusting, slowly, back in.

Lyra opened her legs wider, grasped his biceps tighter and realized how much she loved this connection, this closeness with him.

"But I've got you now," Dion said, lifting off her to grasp both her legs, placing her ankles on his shoulders. "And I'm never letting you go."

God, she hoped not!

His pace picked up considerably and a light sheen of sweat covered Lyra's body. When he turned her onto her stomach and entered her again she screamed into the pillow, her fingers fisting handfuls of the sheets beneath her. Dion's rugged voice was in her ear, telling her how good she felt, how much he loved being inside her. Lyra was going crazy. He'd stroked one pleasure point and found another and now she thought she would simply explode. When he pulled her up onto her knees she couldn't hold back any longer. Thrusting back to meet his every stroke she called his name.

He joined her with a loud moan of his own and they both collapsed on the bed as their ultimate release took over.

Chapter 13

"I have to go," Lyra said when he caught her trying to sneak out.

Dion knew he'd shocked her when she went to stand after tying her shoes and he was sitting on the edge of the bed staring at her intently.

"It's just about dawn, you might as well stay," he said.

"I'd rather not be coming into the house when your parents are sitting down to breakfast."

"You're an adult," he said, standing because she was already heading for the door.

He followed her even though he was naked. After all they'd done hours ago—and what he'd intended to do when they awoke this morning—he wasn't feeling terribly modest.

"Wait," he said, grabbing her by the arm. "Just wait

a minute. You're running out of here like you've broken some kind of law."

She stopped but wouldn't look at him. "I don't know how to do this," she admitted. "The morning-after thing, or should I say the hours-after thing. I just don't know how."

"First," Dion said, lifting her chin so she would look at him. "You don't sneak out. That's juvenile. And second, you start by saying good morning." He leaned forward kissing her first on the forehead, then on the tip of her nose, finally on her lips.

"Dion." His name was a sigh instead of the heated request he'd come to love hearing. "I need to figure out how to play this. We need to figure it out. Your parents are going to have questions. Your family."

"Questions about what? We're both consenting adults who consented to making love, finally. What questions would they ask?"

"I live with your parents. They paid for me to go to school. They've taken care of me half my life. This," she said, spreading her arms wide, "looks like I'm repaying them by sleeping with their son. That's not cool."

"What are you talking about? Repaying them? Have they ever asked you for anything, Lyra? You really think they're looking to be repaid for loving you."

"No!" she yelled. "Yes! I mean, see, this is what I'm saying. I don't know what to do next."

"You start by telling Mark the wedding's off. Then we move on with our lives. It's simple."

"It's simple for you, you're Dion Donovan! The world is your oyster, you can and usually do whatever you want, no questions asked."

He didn't like the way this conversation was going,

or the way he was feeling each time she spoke. He'd thought he knew Lyra as well as he knew himself, but Dion had no idea she felt like she owed his family something. Or that he was above any kind of rules or standards.

"Okay, before this gets out of hand, let's take a deep breath." She looked at him like that was the absolute last thing she wanted to do, but she didn't move.

"Why don't we both just go to work and think about this for a couple of hours. We can have dinner tonight and talk about it some more."

She was shaking her head negatively before he even finished speaking.

"I'm having dinner with Mark."

Dion wanted to tell her she was doing no such thing. He wanted to demand she stop seeing Mark immediately. But he knew that wasn't the way to deal with Lyra, especially not in the state she was currently in. Instead he took another deep breath and said, "That's probably a good idea. You take care of your business first, then we'll talk."

"Fine," she said, pulling away from him. "I have to go."

"Wait a second, let me slip something on and I'll walk you out."

She was already fiddling with the locks and pulling the door open. "I'm fine by myself."

With one last look at him Lyra moved into the hallway and was already walking away while Dion stood at the door watching her go. He couldn't very well run after her in the buff, but damn if he didn't want to.

This was not the way he'd envisioned their first morning together, not at all.

* * *

This was so bad.

Two nights ago, when she'd only kissed Dion, Lyra had thought guilt was going to devour her. Now, after she'd slept with him, she was sure the betrayal was spray-painted across her forehead. Pulling the covers over her head, she wanted to stay in the bed, in this room, for the rest of her natural life.

But life being what it is wouldn't allow that.

She had lunch with Regan today and dinner with Mark tonight. Two people Lyra definitely did not want to see. Regan would know something was going on and Mark would certainly suspect. Lately, Mark had been suspecting a lot. Lyra got the impression he might be a little jealous of Dion and the Donovans and she'd been trying really hard to be patient with him about it, but he really needed to get over it. Dion and the Donovans were like family, it was that simple. Okay, maybe Dion wasn't like family any longer, since she'd slept with him.

And boy did she sleep with him.

Her body warmed as she remembered the things they'd done last night. Things she hadn't even considered doing with Mark. Things that even now made her hungry for more.

Crap. How was she going to face anyone today?

Her cell phone rang and Lyra groaned. Who would be calling her at the crack of dawn?

"Hello?" she answered, when she'd finally pushed the blankets off her face and rolled over close enough to the nightstand to grab the phone.

"Ms. Anderson?"

"Yes?"

"This is Dr. Svanna from Cedars Hospital. I'm calling to let you know that your mother checked herself out of the hospital AMA this morning."

"What?"

"Against medical advice. She had breakfast, said she was feeling better and left."

"But what about the poisoning?"

"Turns out the drugs she'd taken were bad, laced with something the lab couldn't figure out. She didn't get much of it, that's why it only made her sick and didn't do any permanent damage. But the plan was to get her into rehab later today. I guess she didn't like that idea," Dr. Svanna said with a touch of hopelessness.

Lyra sighed. "I guess not."

"You know rehabilitation is only going to work when it's what she wants. I've seen this scenario too many times to count. You wanting her to get better isn't going to make it happen."

"I know," Lyra said, because she'd heard this all before. "Thanks for calling, doctor. I appreciate it."

"No problem."

Disconnecting the call, Lyra fell back onto her pillows, arm draped over her eyes. When would she learn? And when would the pain of being helpless subside? Never seemed like the best answer. But she didn't have time to dwell on this part of her life. It wasn't going to change unless she changed it.

Getting out of bed was the first step. Standing beneath the brutally hot spray of the shower was the next. When she was dressed and finally ready to face the world, Lyra decided to be bold and went into the kitchen instead of sneaking out the front door as she'd considered doing.

"Well, hello, stranger." Mr. Bruce looked up from his newspaper as she walked in.

"Good morning," she said reaching for as normal a tone as possible.

"Heading to work?" he asked.

Lyra had opened the refrigerator, finding the container of orange juice, and now searched for a glass. "I sure am. No late mornings for the newbies," she joked.

"You're no newbie. I hear you're doing a great job."

Lyra sipped the juice she'd just poured in her glass. "I'm trying."

Bruce put the paper down. "You're trying to do a lot of things, I hear."

"What?"

"Trying to get married, making me feel like an old man." He chuckled.

"You'll never be an old man, Mr. Bruce." And she meant that. At fifty-nine, Bruce Donovan still went into the office every day, sometimes ten to twelve hours a day. He played golf, traveled extensively with his wife and still managed to be at Sunday dinners with his family.

"Sit down for a minute. I haven't had time to look at you," he said, pulling out the chair next to him.

She should have headed out the front door, Lyra thought as she put her glass on the counter and went to the table to obediently take a seat.

"I look the same as I've always looked," she said trying to keep the mood light.

Bruce shook his head. Behind him the blinds were lifted from the set of six windows, the sunlight glistening off the water poured into the room reminding everyone who entered how beautiful the morning truly was.

"No. You look a little tired."

Lyra drummed her fingers on the table. "Maybe it's the move."

Bruce put his hands over hers. "Maybe you're trying to do too much."

Inhaling deeply, Lyra realized she'd never lied to this man. In the years she'd lived in this house with him she'd always done her best to respect him and his wishes. Lying wasn't something the Donovans condoned. She wasn't going to start now.

"Maybe," she admitted quietly.

"You want to tell me why?"

She really didn't. But she would because it was Mr. Bruce, the only father figure she'd ever known.

"Because I feel like I have to prove something. I have to show you and Ms. Janean that bringing me into your home wasn't a waste of time."

When she looked up at him again he was shaking his head. "You always were older than your time. I used to tell Janean you carried the worries of an adult on your child's shoulders. Now you're an adult and you're still carrying the issues of others with you like baggage."

She shrugged because she didn't really know what to say to that. It wasn't exactly a lie.

"Dion called this morning to check on you. He told me about Paula and her scare last night."

"He shouldn't have," she said, trying to pull her hands away from his. "You've done enough to try and help her. It's my problem now."

Bruce shook his head. "That's where you're wrong, Lyra. It's not your problem. Paula is not your problem. She's known what she was doing to herself for years now. There's nothing you can do that we haven't already tried for your sake. Now you just have to let her walk her own path."

"She's going to kill herself," Lyra said, tears stinging her eyes. She didn't want them to fall, didn't want to sit here and cry to Mr. Bruce about her mother. Again.

"Then that's her choice. There's nothing you can do if that's what she wants. You're killing yourself trying to save her."

"What else am I supposed to do? She's my mother!" Lyra shouted because that felt better than crying.

"You're supposed to live your life. Deep down that's what Paula really wants for you. She wants you to have the life she couldn't give you, the one she didn't have. That's why she never took you from us."

"She never let you adopt me, either."

"No. Because she needed to stay connected to you. I think that's what's kept her alive all this time. But Paula knows what she hasn't been to you. She knows you were better off here with us. Now it's your turn to do what's best for you."

"I'm trying."

"Are you? Is this Mark person the man you really want to marry?"

There was something about this question, something about the way Mr. Bruce had said it, that had Lyra looking at him, wondering.

"Mark has been good to me over the years."

"That's something you'd say about a puppy, not a man you're about to commit the rest of your life to."

She shrugged. "I don't know what else to say."

"And that alone should have you questioning your decision."

Lyra lifted her hands to cover her face, afraid the torrent of tears she was holding back were going to burst free at any moment. "I feel like I'm making a mess of things, but that's not my intention."

"You know what your problem is, Lyra? You think too much," Bruce said, tapping at her temple until she looked up at him again.

"Stop analyzing and figuring everything you do has a purpose and that purpose has to be known. For once, I think you should follow your heart. Do what you feel is best inside, for you. You might be surprised how good that feels."

He leaned forward, kissing her forehead before he got up to get himself another cup of coffee. "Have a good day at work," he said to her on his way out of the kitchen.

Lyra didn't move. Through blurry eyes she sat looking out the window, replaying the words Mr. Bruce had said to her, noting just how many of them were true.

Chapter 14

Dion had called Lyra twice already. She was ignoring him, of that he was sure. The question was what he planned to do about it. Before he could contemplate that any longer, the door to his office swung open.

In came Katrina in a flurry of long, dark, curly hair, eyelashes and the glitter of diamonds. Her dark eyes fixated on him as high heels and legs that seemed to go on for days marched toward his desk. Behind her a frazzled Jennifer, his assistant, looked ready to kill.

"I can call security, Mr. Donovan," Jennifer said with another glare toward Katrina.

"Don't waste your time," Katrina said without looking back at the other woman. "He's not going to cause a scene by having me thrown out of the building. Are you, Dion baby?"

With a nod Dion sent Jennifer away. When the door

was closed he glared at Katrina Saldana himself, wondering what had ever possessed him to get involved with the gold-digging tramp. Generally, he had better taste than her, but she'd caught him at a weak moment. The night he'd visited the club where she danced was the same night Lyra had emailed him that Mark had proposed to her. Everything inside Dion had spun out of control as he read those words, and he'd been supremely grateful that this time Lyra had decided to tell him her news through email, when all other times it had been via a personal telephone call. Maybe she'd known he wouldn't take the news well. And he hadn't.

He'd spent the night with Katrina, sleeping with her to dull the pain that throbbed in his chest every time he thought of Lyra with Mark. It hadn't really worked. And it wasn't until the next morning that he realized his mistake with Katrina. She was a clinger and she thought she had her hooks in him, a Donovan. He'd known her game that morning and had vowed she'd learn a hard lesson from him. But he'd continued to see her, because truth be told, the vivacious beauty had been good at keeping his mind off Lyra, the woman he thought he'd never have.

Still, the distraction didn't last long. What he felt for Lyra was too deep for even Katrina and all her talents to make disappear.

"What do you want, Katrina?" he said with the impatience he felt. He didn't really have time to deal with her right now. He wanted to talk to Lyra, to make sure they were both on the same page about what happened last night.

Katrina had already taken a seat, crossing her long legs so the short royal blue skirt she wore rode even higher up her thigh. Her blouse was a lighter shade of the color, silk, expensive, just like the jewelry she wore. Dion wondered what man she was swindling money out of now to support her lavish lifestyle. That was one thing he did not do. While he may have enjoyed Katrina's voracious sexual appetite, he'd never promised her any commitment and he'd never, ever given her any money.

"I don't like to be ignored, Dion," she said with her glossed pouting lips. "I just want to talk to you."

"There's nothing else for us to talk about. I told you weeks ago it was over. Case closed."

"Case closed for whom? I have feelings for you, Dion. Are you really going to just toss that out the door? Are you that cruel?"

She batted those fake eyelashes at him as if she really thought it would change his mind. He suspected for some men, it probably worked. But he wasn't some man.

"We had fun and now it's finished. I'm sure you know what that means."

His words struck a chord. He could see the flicker in her eyes, the minute she adjusted the way she sat in the chair and her game plan all at the same time. "What if I'm not finished with you?"

"I don't give a damn," he replied simply.

She let a hand fall to her exposed knee, then slide back up her thigh. He knew the motion, knew what it was supposed to do, but looked back into her eyes without another word. She was a beautiful Colombian woman with a fiery personality and a sultry demeanor. But she wasn't the woman for him.

"Really?" She sat straight up in the chair and glared

back at him. "What would Daddy say if he found out you'd slept with a stripper?"

Dion didn't even blink. "My sex life is my business. There's no threat in telling my father anything, Katrina. Try again."

"No, Dion," she said, standing. "I don't think I'll give you the pleasure just yet." Digging into her purse she pulled out a picture that she tossed in Dion's direction as she made her way to the door. "A picture's worth a thousand words, don't you think?"

By the time Dion picked up the picture Katrina was already leaving his office. He didn't curse, didn't yell for Jennifer to send security to grab that bitch regardless of the scene she'd likely cause. No, Dion only sat back in his chair staring at the picture of Lyra leaving his house last night—or should he say very early this morning. What was Katrina up to?

Chapter 15

Mark canceled dinner, to Lyra's elation. Instead she'd had a nice dinner with Bruce and Janean in the same kitchen where she'd sat crying in the morning.

Her day had been long and grueling. The retake photo session with Vina had gone well, if she didn't count Vina's glaring boyfriend and the snide remarks from other members of her entourage. Vina had been surprisingly sober and offered a much better representation of herself than she had earlier in the week. They'd definitely get a good cover shot from this batch of photos.

Lunch with Regan had been just as she'd suspected—a question-and-answer session in which Regan pumped her for as much information as she could get about her upcoming nuptials.

"What perplexes me is why you aren't more excited,"

Regan had said when they sat on the balcony of Spaga, a new, trendy restaurant that sold the chicken tacos Lyra loved. Regan said she knew the owner but despised him. Still, patronizing his establishment looked good for the Donovans overall, since they planned to feature the African-American owner in *Infinity* in the upcoming months.

"More excited about what? You know I'm not into picking out clothes and matching colors. Catering and flowers and all that other stuff bothers me just as much. I'd be content heading to the courthouse and saying I do," Lyra said flippantly.

"Liar," Regan accused. "You know you want the whole fairy-tale wedding. You're just downplaying it now that it's really here. You remember when we planned our weddings?"

She remembered and wasn't at all shocked that Regan had, too. "That seems like forever ago."

"Yeah, I know. But we were both sure of what we wanted. You said black and white everything. You'd wear a full dress, strapless, lots of lace. I wanted more sparkle and a dress that smoothed over every curve and lots of color. We both wanted to be married outside. Me in a huge park with lots of trees and flowers."

Lyra couldn't help but smile. "I wanted to be married right on the pier in back of the Big House. We'd look out onto the water as we said our vows. Simple, yet touching."

"See, I knew you remembered."

"Sure I remember, but that was long ago. It was the dream of two young girls. We're not those girls anymore."

"Speak for yourself," Regan said with a smile. She

was so pretty with her feisty haircut and alluringly slanted eyes. Lyra knew without a doubt that Regan Donovan would have her dream wedding with all that she'd ever wanted someday. While she, on the other hand, would settle for only what was necessary.

"I'm going to find Mr. Right and have that wedding in the park with all the bling I can manage." Regan laughed. "But first we have to get you down the aisle. Right?"

That was the million-dollar question today. First, Mr. Bruce had asked her if she was sure about marrying Mark, and now Regan was asking that same question. Lyra wouldn't count Dion's questioning of the union, she'd heard all his arguments in the weeks before she returned and again this morning when she'd left his condo. She hadn't talked to him all day, but that hadn't stopped her from thinking about him.

"I want to get married. I want to start a family and do all the things my mother never did for me," she confessed to Regan.

"And you want to do that with Mark?" When Lyra didn't answer right away, Regan kept right on talking. "I'm just asking because he's definitely fine and he's making a boatload of money, but there seems to be something missing between the two of you. I remember when he took you to the prom and you couldn't wait to go home. He looked like he couldn't wait to get you to the nearest hotel, but I knew you'd never go all the way with him on prom night. Then you left town with him and I thought maybe you were okay with him. But I've got to tell you, Lyra. I don't really get that vibe from you two. I don't really feel like you're in love with him."

And this was why she loved Regan, because there

was nothing this woman would not say that she didn't honestly mean. Their friendship was such that they could both be truthful, and Lyra gave a sigh of relief. For months she'd harbored her doubts, letting them float around in her own mind but not daring to voice them. Since being home with the Donovans she'd felt an overwhelming need to purge herself completely.

"I'm not in love with him," Lyra finally admitted. "He's stable and he's good and on the one hand I don't think I should be greedy and ask for more."

"Tell me you're joking," Regan said with a sigh of her own. "Are you kidding me? You deserve to be greedy. You were dealt a crappy hand at life, Lyra. You should be asking for more. Hell, you should be demanding more after all you've been through. Don't settle for this guy just because you feel obligated to him. If he's not the one, toss him aside and wait until you find the one."

Lyra laughed. "That's so easy for you to say. Look at all the options you have. I'm not you, Regan. Sure, I grew up with all of you, but I'm not like you."

"No, you're not. Donovans don't give up, they fight for what they want until they get it. You, on the other hand, haven't learned a thing since living with us. Stand up and take what you want, Lyra. You deserve at least that much."

Their food had come after that and the conversation had thankfully switched to something else. But Regan's words still echoed in her mind. Lyra wasn't in love with Mark, she never had been. All her life she'd only loved one man.

And later that evening, when she looked up from the lounge she'd been sitting in at the pool she saw him walking toward her. Everything inside her leaped for joy, everything except the brain that told her she was treading in unmarked territory. But for the first time in her life, Lyra didn't mind. She wanted the new and unchartered, wanted to feel the rush of an impulsive act, especially one she'd dreamed of for years.

"I called you today," he said the moment he was close enough for her to hear him.

"I know," Lyra replied, lifting herself up off the chair to stand so she could face him.

"We need to talk."

He looked serious in his khaki pants and polo shirt. He looked delicious with the dimming lights from around the pool basking them in a golden haze.

"I don't want to talk," she stated boldly.

"Lyra—" he began, but she cut him off by coming up on tiptoe, wrapping her arms around his neck and pulling his face closer to hers.

"I said, I don't want to talk."

When her lips touched his, fire instantly ignited throughout her body. Lyra pressed closer to him, took the kiss deeper and was rewarded by his arms wrapping around her lifting her until her feet no longer touched the floor.

She wrapped her legs around his waist, sighed when his hands cupped her bottom, kneaded and rubbed while their tongues continued to duel.

He was moving. Lyra could feel them both moving but didn't open her eyes to see where. She heard what sounded like a door opening then closing but kept her lips on his. When her back hit a wall, she gasped and opened her eyes. He'd walked them into the pool house and kicked the door closed behind them. Now his fingers hastily pulled at the bikini top she wore. When his head lowered and his mouth covered one breast she cursed and bucked against him.

"Dion!" His name escaped her lips in a ragged cry.

Again, he wasn't gentle. He didn't whisper any flowery words or romantic preludes, he simply took. And she gave.

Lyra was completely bare at the top and still in his arms. Her own frantic hands tore at his shirt until he leaned back and pulled it over his head. She anxiously leaned forward, kissing his broad shoulders and down to his taut pectorals. His hands were in her hair pulling until her scalp stung as he groaned his pleasure.

In seconds she heard and felt him fiddling with his belt buckle. Her hands raced downward to help him. His pants and underwear slid down and she held his heated length in her hands.

"Dammit! I love when you touch me," he groaned in her ear.

Wrapping her fingers around him and stroking him from the base to the tip Lyra replied, "I love touching you."

With a yank her bikini bottom fell to the floor, her back pressed even harder against the wall. She guided his length to her waiting entrance and gripped his shoulders as he pressed deep inside.

There was nothing but this moment, this feeling, this man. Nothing and everything as he began to move inside her and she rode him with all the pent up desire she'd had for him.

He whispered her name. She whispered his. He took her with a fierce hunger that rivaled even the passion they'd experienced last night. It was as if he owned this part of her, had waited until this very moment to claim what she'd held aside just for him. Lyra wanted to scream her pleasure. She wanted to whimper with the desire she'd always had for this Donovan man. Instead, she matched his fervor with a heat of her own, undulating her hips until they were both breathing heavily, climbing and climbing for the highest release.

"You belong to me." His voice echoed in her ear seconds before his teeth scraped over her lobe. "Say it! Tell me you belong to me!"

Lyra felt like she finally belonged to herself, like this was the defining moment in her life when she had let go and done exactly what she wanted to do, damn the consequences. But there was also a measure of truth to his words. She did belong to Dion, she always had.

"Yes!" was her eventual reply. "I belong to you!"

She held on to him as he pounded deeper and deeper inside her. Her nails dug into his skin as his fingers gripped her bare bottom fiercely.

Lyra felt unstoppable and uncontrollable as Dion pressed her against the wall, taking her like his life depended on it, like *their* lives depended on it.

When her thighs quivered with her release and she kissed down his neck, Dion moaned loudly, tensing inside her before relaxing. He still held her close as they both struggled to take normal breaths.

"I can't go back to the way we were, Lyra," he said into her ear. "I want more from you than friendship."

She didn't speak, only nodded her agreement.

"We can make this work. Nobody knows me the way you do, and vice versa. I think we've always known it would come to this."

The more he talked, the more her heart swelled with love for this man. He'd always been there for her, in every way she'd needed him, at the time she'd needed him. He was her best friend, her confidant, her staunchest supporter. Despite all the rumors about his philandering ways, Lyra always knew there was a part of Dion that belonged only to her. The true and real part of the man every woman in the world wanted to be with but only she knew.

"I don't want to hurt your parents," she admitted finally.

"By telling them you want to be with their son." He chuckled. "I doubt that would hurt them. You know my mom's been trying to marry me off since I graduated from college. I think she'll approve of my choice."

"We'll tell them together?" she asked.

"From this point on we'll do everything together," he vowed, kissing her lips again.

Lyra let herself be captured by that kiss, she let it hold her and soothe all her worries. She was finally getting what she wanted, and she should feel a lot better about it than she actually did. But something deep inside still whispered that happily ever after just wasn't for her.

"I hope he doesn't hurt her," Janean said, standing at the kitchen window watching as Dion and Lyra—wearing only a towel wrapped around her—walked across the lawn toward the back door of the house.

"He's a Donovan, dear. It's not in his genes to hurt a woman," Bruce replied.

"But she's not just any woman."

"No," Bruce agreed. "She's not."

Chapter 16

BETRAYED BY A DONOVAN

"Internet mogul Mark Stanford gives a candid interview about his heartbreak and disappointment in Miami's top family."

Savian read the next few sentences in the article before tossing the paper angrily across the conference room table. His father had called a seven o'clock meeting on Tuesday morning. The paper had been released at six Monday night.

A very somber Parker, a contemplative Sean and an all-out angry Dion sat on one side of the long cherrywood table. On the other side was Savian and Regan. At both heads of the table were Reginald and Bruce. Nobody was smiling.

"Did you sleep with her?" Regan asked, staring at Dion.

Savian scoffed. "What kind of question is that? Of course he didn't. Lyra's family. This is a pack of lies and I say we sue the shirt off this rag of a newspaper to show them not to mess with the Donovans."

"A lawsuit is not the type of publicity the magazine needs right now," Sean said, slowly sitting up in his chair and resting his elbows on the table.

"I can't believe Stanford would give this interview," Parker spoke up. "But a lot of what he's saying about the family is dead on. He could only have gotten that information from Lyra. That means there's no doubt he's doing the talking."

"But why?" Reginald asked. "What does he have to gain from putting this information out there? The wedding's still on, right?"

All eyes rested on Dion. "You have to ask Lyra about her wedding plans," he said simply. Then when he saw a few raised brows he cleared his throat and figured he'd better give a little more information, even though he'd promised Lyra they'd tell everyone together.

"Stanford's not entirely wrong. There's something going on between Lyra and me."

"What the hell?" Savian yelled.

Reginald shook his head and Sean squeezed the bridge of his nose. Bruce simply looked at his son.

"Something like what?" Regan demanded. "Don't mess with her, Dion. She's not like those other tramps you have in and out of your life."

"She's right, Dion." Reginald backed his daughter's statement up with a grim nod. "She's like family, for goodness' sake. You couldn't find anyone else to sleep with?"

"It's not like that!" Dion yelled, supremely pissed off that his family seemed to have such a low opinion of him. "There's been something—and by something I mean feelings—between us for a while now. We've just had the chance to act on them since she came back. And I don't have to sit here and explain my personal life at a business meeting."

"Son," Bruce said quietly. "This is family, and the Donovan family always comes first, before any type of business. I think what we're all trying to figure out is if this 'something' is serious? Does Lyra share your feelings?"

Dion stood. "I'm not going to sit here and discuss what's personal between Lyra and me."

"And it doesn't really matter," Sean interjected. "The fact is Stanford leaked this story to the press for a reason. It's obvious he's trying to discredit us, but what does he have to gain from it? We're not poaching on his business and I'd think any other man would be too embarrassed to admit his fiancée is stepping out on him. We need to figure out why he did this."

Dion didn't miss a beat. From the moment he saw the article he'd had her name in the back of his mind, right along with the photo of Lyra she'd slipped him. "Katrina Saldana," he said finally.

"Who?" Savian asked.

"The professional gold digger who stays in the tabloids for one reason or another," Regan volunteered. "She was Dion's flavor of the month a while back."

Dion looked at Regan shaking his head. "Nobody in this room is answering for their personal life. But I'll go along, since it seems my business has seeped into the company. Yes, I dated Katrina Saldana. It wasn't one of my smarter decisions, but I ended it months ago. She's not real happy with that decision."

Regan continued, "I'll bet that's an understatement. Saldana is notorious for hooking up with rich and famous men. Her eye always seems to be on the money prize."

"But she's a looker, that's for sure," Parker added.

"So you think this woman may be in cahoots with Stanford?" Bruce asked.

Dion nodded. "She knows I'm seeing Lyra. I wouldn't put anything past her."

"Maybe she thought if Stanford went public you'd be so disgraced you'd leave Lyra alone," Sean replied.

"Doesn't mean he'd look her way again," Savian said.

"The bottom line is damage control. Should there be any?" Reginald asked.

Bruce surprised everyone with his answer. "No," he said simply. "Dion's personal life is his own concern. This is a tabloid rag that has minor circulation but doesn't hold much credence with anyone who has an ounce of sense. As a corporation I say we ignore it for the vicious rumors that it usually is. And Dion will handle the rest."

Slipping his hands into his pockets, Dion nodded. "I certainly will."

"Are you kidding me?" Lyra said the moment she stormed into Mark's office, dropping the newspaper onto his desk and standing with her hands on both hips. "Since when do we air our personal issues in the press?"

Mark didn't even look down at the paper. "Since you

started sleeping with the man you've always called a 'brother.'"

"This is low, Mark. I planned to talk to you about Dion."

"When? Before or after the wedding?"

Lyra couldn't argue with his logic there. For all intents and purposes she had cheated on her fiancé, no matter that her heart had never been in this relationship in the first place.

"I was going to talk to you last night, but you canceled our date. Now, it appears you were having me followed all along. I guess I was actually the last to know we had trust issues in this relationship."

"Don't come in here talking to me about trust. I've never trusted the Donovans and I've always been honest with you about that. Since you seem to be so in love with that family, it stands to reason I'd want my own assurances."

"Assurances of what? That I care about the family that raised me, that gave me everything I ever dreamed of? Your jealousy of them has always been unfounded. And what did you find out by following me? Nothing. You saw me leaving my best friend's house and that means I'm sleeping with him?"

"I saw you taking care of that pitiful junkie of a mother of yours and then running to that playboy who thinks his bank account can buy him any and everything he wants! I saw the woman that was supposed to be committed to me still chasing a past better left alone. That's what I saw, Lyra!"

"First of all, you don't get to talk about my mother to me. Ever!" she said vehemently. "And furthermore, if I turned to my friends instead of you, whose fault is that?

You've never shown an ounce of compassion where my mother is concerned, nor have you lifted one of your manicured fingers to help her or anybody else for that matter. You're a selfish bastard, Mark Stanford!"

He tossed his head back and laughed. "And you're a naive dreamer. Do you think Donovan is going to marry you, Lyra? You're nothing to him. No, I'll correct that. You're like the help, the very attractive help, and he can't help but indulge himself. But he won't stay committed to you any more than he has to any other woman. You have no idea what he's been doing these past ten years or what he'll continue to do."

"And you never had a clue of who or what I am," she said sadly. It was all clear to her now, the reason she could never really let herself fall completely for Mark Stanford. He was the perfect package, on the outside. But Lyra had always suspected there was something else. Her guilt over thinking of Dion while she was with Mark probably masked it, but now she saw it and him for what they really were.

"If he thinks I'm the attractive help, what do you think I was? Apparently my drug-addicted mother is beneath your standards, so what was I? A pity project? A jab at the Donovans you say I love so much? It's obvious you never really loved me, so what was the purpose in being with me, Mark?"

For a minute he looked shocked at her words, then he covered it smoothly with that smile she'd seen him give his colleagues. He sat back in his chair and folded his hands together as if contemplating what he would say to her next.

"You know what, it doesn't really matter. You are and will always be a pathetic loser trying to be something you're not. No matter where I came from or what unsightly elements I've endured throughout my life, I'm still a good person and that counts for something. In your most expensive suit and with all the money in the world you will never deserve me."

She'd turned to leave when she heard him laughing behind her.

"He'll toss you out like the trash," he called after her.

Lyra stopped, turned to face him once more and laughed herself. "Like the trash you've been sleeping with," she said with a nod to the spot of smudged lipstick on his collar.

Chapter 17

"It figures the moment I think I'm taking control of my life everything spirals out of control," Lyra said dropping onto the couch at Dion's condo. She'd come here straight from work after receiving his text that he'd left the office early.

Dion took a sip from his glass of what Lyra knew would be rum and coke. Approaching her, he gave her the glass of red wine he'd poured and sat beside her when she took it from him.

"It's nothing we can't handle," he told her. Always the optimist, she thought.

"I've never been in the tabloids," Lyra confessed. "I don't like it."

"Nobody likes being in the news, especially when they're being falsely accused."

"But am I falsely accused? I was engaged to Mark when I slept with you. There's no denying that fact."

"But neither me nor my family betrayed Stanford. He was never anything to us, not family and not an employee. How could we betray him? And either way, the paper has a reputation. The majority of the sane world won't believe a word it says."

"And the insane world will believe it all." She sighed.

"Come on, put it out of your mind."

"How do you do that?" she asked. "How do you take this like it's nothing more than an unsightly pimple and move on?"

Dion shrugged. "I'm used to it. You have to be in my position."

"I've never been in your position. Until now."

He emptied his glass, sat it on one of the cube tables and looked at her, putting a hand on her knee. "Listen, Lyra, when you have money and notoriety everybody wants a piece of you. Whether that piece is a look into your life through a tacky tabloid or it's on a terribly scripted reality show, people will buy the paper and they'll watch the show. It feeds into that small, curious part of them that wants to learn everything about someone they'll never really know at all."

"I don't know why, but I understood exactly what you just said." She smiled at him.

"That's because you, unlike the people buying that tabloid and poring over every word it says at this very moment, know me very well."

When he leaned forward to kiss her lips, Lyra closed her eyes momentarily. She let the intimate moment linger through the bad day she'd had.

"I could kiss you for hours," he said, his lips touching hers once more.

"And I could let you," she replied. "But I should probably go."

"What? Are you on some kind of curfew now?"

He moved back a fraction and she took a sip of her wine. "I've been trying to reach my mom."

Dion's look sobered. "I thought you had her checked into rehab after the poison scare."

"She left the hospital before they could transfer her." She hated admitting that, even to Dion.

He inhaled deeply and let the breath out slowly. "You tried her cell?"

"Going straight to voice mail."

"Where'd you pick her up the other night?"

"South. Near the old neighborhood."

Dion stood and looked back at her. "Let's go."

"Where are we going?"

"I'm not letting you go riding around that neighborhood by yourself. You want to find Paula, we'll do it together."

"She's *my* mother," Lyra said coming to her feet. "I should go alone."

"That's not going to happen. So you've got five minutes to decide if you want to go get some dinner or look for *your* mother. Either way, I'm driving."

An hour and a half later Lyra ran her fingers through her hair and sighed with frustration. "She's not at any of her usual hangouts."

"Paula's resourceful. She'll find someplace to sleep and she'll take care of whatever she needs."

"That's what I'm afraid of," Lyra said, then quickly looked over at Dion.

He was driving his black Lexus LX with a look just as intent as hers. Not one word of complaint had been uttered from his mouth no matter how many run-down houses she asked him to stop at. And he never let her walk in one of them alone.

Lyra figured now would be the time he'd give her the lecture about trying to save her mother being a lost cause. But he remained quiet.

"Go ahead and say it," she prompted.

"Say what?" He looked at her quizzically as he turned the next corner.

"Tell me I'm wasting my time. That my mother is never going to change unless she wants to. That I'm fighting a losing battle."

He shook his head. "Why tell you what you already know?"

"Because you've been doing that for years now." She looked out the window then. "I just never listen."

"And that's one of the reasons I admire you so much."

"What?" she asked, turning to him again.

"You're loyal to a fault. No matter what Paula's done in the past, no matter what she does to you now, you won't turn your back on her. You love her in spite of who and what she is."

"I don't know how to do anything else."

He reached a hand over the console and squeezed her shoulder. "That's because it's who you are. No matter what I might think about the situation, don't ever doubt your feelings or your instincts. You do what's right for you."

"Okay," she said quietly. A wash of feelings hit her

at that moment, hard and fast enough to have her shaking in her seat. She folded her arms and looked out the window again so Dion wouldn't notice, but she was still quivering a bit when he turned onto the bridge.

"Where are we going now?" she asked finally.

"I'm hungry. You're hungry. We're going to have dinner, then go home. I'll call some people and give them Paula's description. We'll find her tomorrow. All right?"

Lyra nodded, eternally grateful for this man. Her best friend. And now her lover.

Chapter 18

When the Donovans threw a party it was more like a production. The gorgeously scenic Four Seasons Hotel in Miami Beach set the stage for this year's Children With Disabilities Wish Upon a Star Ball. In the Grand Ballroom, no less, calla lily and hydrangea centerpieces reached from crystal vases toward the ceiling in opulent sprays. Shimmering gold lights illuminated the room, while sparkling china dishes lined cream-colored table linens.

In the pre-event room, early-arriving guests were treated to a magnificent view of the blue-tinted Miami skyline and shimmering moonlit waters. The bars were open and drinks were flowing. Hostesses wearing pins with the Donovan Children With Disabilities Foundation logo mingled throughout the room, making sure all the guests felt welcome and appreciated.

The guest list included everyone from politicians to dignitaries, movie stars to music-industry execs and, of course, the Donovans. This year their family also welcomed Paul and Noreen Lakefield of the Lakefield Galleries. Noreen Lakefield had recently partnered with Alma Donovan to create Karing For Kidz, a program to help support the street children of South America as well as the orphanages in the United States.

One of the Lakefield daughters, Deena, had married into the Donovan family, so she was also in attendance with her husband, Max.

No party could be complete without the remaining Las Vegas Donovans, Henry and Everette, who were brothers of Bruce and Reginald, along with their wives. The Triple Threat Donovans—Linc, Trent and Adam— were also in attendance. The family had truly shown up to lend their support for this yearly event.

And as Lyra walked in on Dion's arm, she felt only slightly overwhelmed.

Dion wore a tailor-made Versace tuxedo, black with a white shirt, his silver-and-black vest adding just a touch of glitz to his stately appearance. He looked picture-perfect with his cleanly shaven face and close-cropped hair.

Regan had picked out Lyra's dress. They were both wearing CK Davis originals, knowing that Adam and his wife, the designer Camille Davis Donovan, would be here tonight. Lyra's was an elegant pink floor-length satin and chiffon gown that made her feel like a princess. The tight bodice and plunging V-neck gave her breasts a voluptuous appearance she'd never known she longed for, while the chiffon swept around her legs in feathery wisps. At her neck she wore a diamond choker with matching earrings and bracelet that had been a graduation gift from Bruce and Janean.

Regan lit up the entire room in her stunning strapless gold floor-length satin dress. She didn't have a date and didn't really seem to care as she made her way toward Lyra and Dion.

"Fabulous!" she cooed the minute she was close enough. Reaching out her hands she touched Lyra's shoulders and turned her around. "I knew this was perfect for you. Don't you agree, Dion?"

He'd told her the second she'd walked down the steps and stopped in front of him in the foyer of the Big House that she looked beautiful, but Lyra had the distinct impression he was talking about more than the dress. Even now when he looked at her again, there was something in his eyes that went beyond what he was seeing physically. She felt it deeper than that and warmed all over.

"It's a great dress and she looks stunning in it" was his reply.

"Oooh, stunning. I don't think I've ever heard him use that word," Regan said with a wiggle of her eyebrows to Lyra.

"Stop teasing," Lyra admonished and stepped out of Regan's grasp. "Now, you look gorgeous. That color is almost glowing on you."

"I know. I love it and it fits me perfectly. I can't wait to see Camille to let her know how much I appreciate all the dresses she sent for us to try on."

"Yes, I must thank her, too, for the four hours you had me locked in your bedroom trying on one dress after another," Lyra said.

Regan waved a hand. "Oh, you loved it. And you

look great. Now you two mingle. There's tons of media here tonight."

"And we could certainly use some good media," Savian said soberly as he came to join them. He, too, looked GQ handsome with his perfectly fitting tuxedo, expertly clipped goatee and somber eyes.

Lyra instantly felt guilty. "I apologize for Mark's story," she said instinctively.

Dion frowned and Savian grumbled. "What are you apologizing for? You can't help he's an ass. I'm just glad you found out before it was too late."

Savian's words were meant to make Lyra feel better, she knew. But she didn't. She hated that her lack of honesty with Mark had brought any harm to the Donovans.

"He just shouldn't have done it," she answered.

Dion took her hand, brought the back to his lips and kissed. "And there was nothing you could have done to stop him. But it's fine. I told you we would handle it."

She nodded, staring into his eyes and feeling the confidence and adoration she'd always longed for. "You did tell me that."

"So the rumors are true," a female voice said from behind and Lyra wanted to crawl into a corner and hide.

Instead she stood tall beside Dion as he pulled her even closer.

"Good evening, Mom, Dad." He leaned forward to kiss his mother's cheek, then was right back beside Lyra.

"Hello, Ms. Janean," Lyra said nervously. Then she managed a smile. "Hi, Mr. Bruce."

"Lyra, my girl, you're a beauty," Bruce said, pulling her away from Dion to give her a hug. "And you've been keeping secrets from me," he whispered into her ear.

"I'm sorry," she said as he pulled away.

"Nonsense. I want you happy. That's all that matters." Bruce's words made Lyra feel a fraction better.

However, the way Janean was still looking from her to Dion had her knees knocking slightly.

"I wonder which one of you I should strangle first," Janean said finally.

"I'll take the brunt of that," Dion said valiantly.

"You'll both take it," she snapped. "If there's one thing I don't tolerate it's secrecy. Did you think your father and I were blind all these years?"

"What do you mean?" Dion asked.

"We knew there was something going on between you two," Janean responded.

"And frankly we were getting tired of waiting for you to catch up," Bruce added.

"But how?" Lyra said, hating that Regan was smiling at her and Savian was even looking a little amused.

"Like I said, we're not blind." Then Janean hugged Lyra close. "Why do you think I wanted you to stay at the house and not move in with that Mark character? I knew you just needed some more time to get it together."

Amazed at how all this seemed to be going on around her without her having a clue, Lyra could only laugh. "I can't believe this."

"I know," Janean said, moving away from Lyra to flatten her palms on the lapels of Dion's tux. "I didn't figure my son to be that slow to make a move."

"Maybe he's losing his touch in his old age," Savian suggested, earning a glare from Dion.

"Don't count on it," was Dion's reply about a second

before he pulled Lyra into his arms and kissed her full on the mouth in front of everyone.

She supposed she should have been embarrassed, at least a little bit. Instead Lyra was warm all over and probably glowing to everyone else as Dion slowly released her but kept his arms around her waist. Looking up at him she wished they were alone, but appreciated the family that surrounded them with their love and blessings. This hadn't turned out the way she'd expected. The revelation of her and Dion being together was actually better than she could have ever imagined.

"Long time, no see, cousin," Trent Donovan said reaching out to shake Dion's hand.

"Same here. You're looking good," Dion replied, giving his cousin the once-over in his tuxedo. "You clean up well. The last time I saw you, your team was investigating some family just south of here."

Trent, part owner of D&D Investigations and ex-Navy Seal, nodded his head. "Right. Bailey and Sam Desdune were helping with that case. We never found the missing child."

"Sorry to hear that." Children were a soft spot for the Donovan family, as evidenced by the ballroom full of Donovan family members and all their supporters.

"It happens," Trent said with a shrug. "But it makes me keep mine a little closer, you know what I mean?"

Trent had married model Tia St. Claire and together they'd had a son, Trevor. It hadn't been until lately that Dion had begun thinking of starting his own family.

"I know exactly what you mean," he said, glancing around the room hoping to catch a glimpse of Lyra. She'd gone off with Regan and Camille Donovan to talk about fashion shows and layouts for the magazine. But that had been a while ago.

"I hear there've been some rumblings going on out here in the papers," Trent said, lifting a glass of champagne from one of the many trays full of them moving about the room.

"Good news travels fast," Dion replied dryly.

"Come on, we're family. You know I keep my eye on things," Trent said. "Besides, D&D Investigations has been keeping tabs on that Saldana woman for a while now. I sent you an email about her last week."

"You did?" Dion was notoriously bad about checking his email, especially since Lyra was now here and he didn't have to wait to hear from her via the internet.

"As soon as I came across pictures of you and her together I figured I'd give you a heads-up. She's got some pretty unsavory friends."

"I don't doubt that."

"I'm glad you seem to have made a much better pick."

Dion smiled. "Much better. Besides, she was just a distraction."

"A costly one. She's fleeced more than one rich guy in her time. You seem to have been her youngest endeavor."

"Really? I knew she had dollar signs in her eyes, but I wasn't aware it was a full-time occupation."

"It is." Trent laughed. "There are a lot of them out there. It's like a profession now, to be a gorgeous woman looking for the next paycheck in a rich man's bed. I even have pics of her with your lady's ex."

That immediately had Dion's attention. "Katrina's been with Mark Stanford?"

Trent nodded. "She has. And both of them were seen recently in a not-so-glamorous neighborhood in Miami. Not real sure yet why. But since we're tracking Saldana's movements, I'm sure it'll come up sooner rather than later."

Something like dread shivered down Dion's spine. "They were both in this neighborhood?"

"We've got pictures of the car, registered to Stanford. Both of them were in the car. Looks like they made some kind of drug buy, which isn't all that surprising. Then Stanford went into a house and came back out."

"Do you have the address of the house?"

"I do." Trent reached into his pocket and pulled out his cell phone. After a few minutes of what Dion supposed was scrolling through files he read off an address.

Dion cursed, his fists clenching at his sides.

"I've got to find Lyra" was all he said before moving through the crowd of people.

Chapter 19

"Excuse me a moment," Lyra said stepping away from Regan and Camille, who were still standing on the balcony where they'd been talking for the past twenty minutes.

These shoes were killing her feet, and Lyra needed a slight reprieve from the endless fashion talk. She moved through the entryway where they'd first come into the ballroom and down a small hallway to the bathroom, pushing through the door without hesitation. After using the facilities, washing her hands and fixing her makeup, she sat on one of the lounge chairs in the front of the restroom and slipped out of her shoes. Looking down, she sighed at how such a beautiful creation, five-inch-heeled silver strappy sandals that had the barest hint of sparkle on them, could be so painful. With a groan she let her toes uncurl and appreciated the moment of silence.

It didn't last long.

"Aren't you a sight?" a female voice taunted.

Positive the person wasn't talking to her, Lyra cracked one eye open. The second she saw the red satin draped over a luscious figure, dark eyes and even darker hair hanging across one shoulder in a seductive array of curls, she sat up.

"Do I know you?" Lyra asked, even though she had a pretty good idea just who this attractive woman was.

"You certainly know my man" was her reply.

"Excuse me?"

"Don't play coy. It's not cute, especially not on you," she said, coming closer to stand in front of Lyra.

Feeling a little intimidated, Lyra stood, even though without her heels she wasn't quite eye to eye with the woman, or should she say Katrina Saldana.

"You think you've got him don't you?" Katrina asked.

"If you're talking about Dion, you should know that nobody has him. Ever. He's his own man."

Katrina nodded, folding her arms over her chest. "I have him and something else you don't," she stated.

Bending over but still keeping her eye on Katrina, Lyra slipped her feet back into her shoes, feeling a lot better now that she was taller. "Look, whatever was between you two is over. I don't have time to conversate over the past."

She moved to walk away but Katrina grabbed her by the arm.

"Oh, don't think you're getting off that easy. I have a few things to say to you, little miss thing."

"My name is Lyra."

"Your name should be trashy wannabe." Katrina

laughed. "Did you really think Dion was going to get rid of all this for you? You're not in his league, not by a long shot. It would make sense for you to just go back to the hood where you're from."

Something about the way she'd said that last sentence had Lyra looking closely at this woman. She had the audacity to call Lyra a wannabe when everything about her screamed fake, from her painted glue-on nail tips to the breasts that just about fell out of the halter of her gown to the lashes that were extraordinarily long and curled.

"You don't know anything about me," Lyra shot back.

"Oh, don't I? Your boyfriend has loose lips," she said waiting a beat for Lyra to understand who she was talking about. "Especially in bed."

"Tramp!" Lyra said, and took another step to leave.

"He told me about your poor drug-addicted mother. He really only tried to help her, you know. A quick death is much better than the prolonged drug use, wouldn't you say?"

The muted pink-and-gold décor of the restroom swirled in Lyra's vision. What was this bitch trying to say?

"I'm leaving," she said instead.

"Yes, you should leave. You should go and try to save your mother again. She's here you know, down the hall guzzling all the booze she can for free. I think she'll be passing out in another few minutes or so. Not a real good look for the Donovans on their big night, is it?"

Lyra didn't say another word, just headed for the door.

"Oh, and Lyra?" Katrina called from behind.

"When you're scraping your mother up off the floor, say goodbye to Dion. There's no way he's going to stay with you when he finds out I'm carrying his child."

Lyra's feet couldn't move fast enough. The hemline of the dress she'd loved so much now swirled around her legs, trapping her so that she couldn't go as fast as she wanted to. The bars were only set up in the pre-function room. Inside the ballroom drinks were passed on trays throughout the sit-down meal and now the music hour. If her mother was here, Katrina had been right, she'd be at the bar.

Lyra's goal was to get her mother out of here as soon as possible. The last thing the Donovans needed was another scandal because of her. But as she moved her heart hammered in her chest, her temples throbbing at Katrina's parting words. Was she really carrying Dion's baby?

A loud voice tore her attention away from the question.

"I ain't finished yet," the slurred female voice said.

Lyra almost groaned with dread. "Excuse me," she said, pushing past a couple more people.

"Ma'am, I think you've had enough," a male voice was now saying, raised above the slight murmur of conversation.

Lyra moved faster.

"You don't know me. I can shrink as much as I want to," Paula stated loudly.

"I'm calling security," the man, Lyra could now see was one of the hosts hired by the Donovans, said determinedly.

"It's all right," she said, putting a hand on the man's

arm to stop him from going to do just that. "I'll take her home."

"But Ms. Anderson," he started to say. "This is a situation for security to handle. You should go back into the ballroom."

Lyra frowned momentarily. He thought she belonged in the ballroom with the rest of these rich and classy people, while Paula, her mother—who'd mysteriously found another glass—was letting the liquid slosh over the rim as she tried to hold herself upright and drink at the same time.

"No. This is my situation to handle," Lyra said slowly. "Come on," she said to her mother, taking the glass from her hands.

"That's mine. Get your own!" she exclaimed.

"No! You've had enough," Lyra said, wrapping her arm around Paula's waist. "We're leaving."

"I ain't ready to leave."

"I didn't ask you if you were ready. You're either leaving with me and I'll take you home, or the police are coming up here to haul you away in cuffs. And I'm not bailing you out of jail."

"You ain't my mama."

"No. I'm not," Lyra said, attempting to steer Paula toward the hallway and the elevators.

"I'm *your* mama, you should be listening to me."

"Yes, you are my mother," Lyra said grimly, still trying to get them away from the party. This was her mother and this was her life. There was no use in her trying to convince herself any differently.

"Lyra!"

She heard her name and turned at the voice.

"What happened?" Dion asked.

Behind him was Sean, looking angry as he saw Paula.

"Nothing. Go back inside. I'll take care of her," she said.

"I don't need nobody to take care of me," Paula replied leaning into Lyra's back. "I can get home by myself. Let me hold your keys."

Lyra did have her car keys in her purse. While she'd come to the ball with Dion, he'd brought her car over earlier today. He was taking the Lakefields directly to the airport after the ball, a favor to his mother. So Lyra was going to drive directly to his condo and wait for him.

"I'll drive you home," she said to her mother through clenched teeth.

"No. I'll take her home," Dion said stepping closer to them.

Lyra put up her hand stopping him. "I have to do this. You guys go back in before she makes any more of a scene. No more bad press, remember," she said, imploring Sean to get Dion out of here.

"Let her go," Sean said, grabbing Dion's arm.

"Let me go, dammit!" Paula yelled, snatching Lyra's purse from her shoulder. "I'm sick of all y'all stuck-up asses!"

Paula had grabbed the purse and spun away before Lyra could grab her.

"I've gotta go," she said, looking up to Dion. "Maybe you should go and find Katrina. She has something to tell you."

"Katrina? She's here?"

Lyra didn't wait to answer his question. Her chest hurt, her head hurt. The room was spinning as if she'd been the one drinking. She turned and ran to the elevator slamming the palm of her hand into the button praying it would appear quickly.

Chapter 20

"What the hell are you doing here?" Dion asked Katrina the moment he turned around and saw her standing there wearing a smirk that spoke volumes.

"I was invited" was her reply. "Besides, we need to talk."

Dion nodded. He wanted to talk to her all right. "Out here," he said, nodding toward the balcony. When Sean gave him a concerned look Dion nodded at him, too, letting him know he had this under control.

"I'll be right here," Sean told him with a warning glance to Katrina.

"Oh, what're you, his bodyguard now? That's funny, the strong, silent Donovan trying to protect the gorgeous, rowdy one," Katrina said with a laugh.

Dion grabbed her by the arm. "Let's go."

"Don't manhandle me," she said when they were

out on the balcony and she could pull out of his grasp. "This is all your fault."

"My fault? How do you figure that?"

"You're the one sleeping with the help when you know you should have left her and her trashy mother in L.A."

"Really? And where should I have left you, Katrina? Swinging on that pole with your breasts out for everyone to see? Or maybe I should have left you at the bar smiling over a drink you couldn't afford to pay for?"

For a second she seemed startled. Maybe it was his tone. Dion rarely yelled. He had a temper but didn't lose it with women, usually only in the boardroom. But this female had gone too far.

"I'm better for you than she is," Katrina said, lifting her head higher.

"Why, because you're used to sleeping with rich men for money?"

"Don't talk to me like I'm some cheap slut. I offered you my heart, my soul. Everything, and you tossed it away for her!" Katrina was screaming now, her hair blowing wildly in the cool breeze that had just seemed to pick up.

"I never asked you for anything. In fact, I never wanted anything from you but what I got. It was sex, Katrina. That's all you were good for."

"You bastard!" she said, lifting a hand to slap him.

Dion caught her wrist, squeezing it until she gasped. Then he pulled her close to his chest and glared down into her face. "You listen to me. I know exactly what you've done. I have pictures of you and Stanford making a buy, then delivering that poison to Paula Anderson. It's enough to get you put away for attempted murder."

"What?" she gasped.

"Then I have information on you extorting money from men. Another couple of years you can spend behind bars."

"No." She shook her head. "You don't know anything. Let me go!"

"Oh, I'm going to let you go, all right. I'm going to let you go and you're going to walk back into that ballroom where the police are waiting to take you away."

"That's impossible!"

Dion pushed her away from him, watched her stumble and didn't give a damn if she fell flat on her ass. "You haven't learned a thing in all your research of me. Anything's possible when you're a Donovan," he told her, then stalked off the balcony.

He hadn't really called the police, but Trent was here, and he was a licensed private investigator with an active investigation on Katrina. He could take her into custody, then deliver her to the police station. And Dion could go after Lyra.

"I can shrive," Paula said, leaning over the console in Lyra's silver Audi A7.

"You can barely see. Get over there and put your seat belt on," Lyra said angrily. She was pissed that her mother was yet again drunk and that she'd had the audacity to show up at the ball. And she was livid with Dion for sleeping with such a horrid slut as Katrina Saldana. And she was disappointed in herself for believing that finally she would have her happily ever after. Katrina was probably right, Dion wouldn't change. And if Katrina was carrying his baby, Lyra didn't even want to deal with that type of baby-mama drama, which was almost definitely promised in this case.

"You should have stayed wherever you've been hiding out these past few days," she told her mother.

"What? You can't talk to me like that. I'm the mutha."

"You're something, I'll say that." Tears stung Lyra's eyes as she drove, her hands sweating over the steering wheel.

"You checked out of the hospital when you told me you'd stay. I looked for you and looked for you. I should have known you'd be all right. And now you show up here to get drunk. How could you embarrass me like that?"

"You. You. You. Always thinking of yourself. Brat. That's what you are, a brat," she said, spitting across the dashboard as she did. "Let me out of this car. I can walk."

"Dion said you could take care of yourself. I should have listened," Lyra spoke more to herself then to Paula.

"You still hung up on that boy with the cute face. He ain't no good for you." Paula reached out a hand and slapped it on Lyra's bare shoulder. "Now that other dude you was sleeping with, that Mike, he's got class. And he's got connections, too. Got me some stuff so good I felt like I was flying for days."

"What?" Lyra said looking over at her mother. "Are you talking about Mark?"

"Mark. Mike. Mr. Magoo. Whoever. He got some good stuff. You know what, just drop me off at his house. I need him to hook me up again."

"When exactly did Mark hook you up?" Lyra asked, fear and dread gripping her heart in a tight grasp.

"It wasn't his fault that night. I had some other stuff,

too. Them docs don't know nothing. I wasn't no poisoned. Dumbasses."

"Mark gave you drugs that night I came to get you?"

"He knows how to take care of a woman. You ask me, that's the one you need to be chasing. Not too-good-rich-boy back there." She waved a hand and it smacked against the window. "It's hot in here, roll this window down."

"I can't believe this. Mark," Lyra whispered as she turned another corner.

"I said roll this window down," Paula was saying, banging on the window.

But Lyra wasn't paying her request any attention. Lyra was thinking of all that had just happened, all that had been happening since she came home. Katrina said she slept with Mark. Paula just said Mark gave her drugs. Who the hell was Mark Stanford and why did he pick her? He was a bastard, that's what he was! Giving her mother drugs when he knew how long Lyra had been trying to get her clean. And sleeping with that bitch Katrina, too. How dare he have her followed when he was cheating as well as trying to kill her mother.

"I'm hot!" Paula yelled.

"Shut up!" Lyra yelled back. "Put your damned seat belt on and shut up! I'm sick of doing this with you, sick of running around in circles over and over again. I'm just tired of it! And this is the last time. Either you decide to get clean or I'm through with you. I'm not going to spend the rest of my life picking you up off the floor, watching you puke your brains out or almost die in the emergency room. I'm just not going to keep doing this!"

"Don't you yell at me!" Paula was reaching over

again, this time pushing Lyra's head to the side. "I'll beat your ass!" she yelled and pushed Lyra again.

Lyra elbowed her, trying to push her back. "Put the damned seat belt on like I told you," she said.

Paula didn't listen, just lunged at Lyra again. "I don't have to listen to you!"

"You have to while you're in my car. Sit back!"

"No! Pull over! Let me out of here! I'll have you ar-reshed!"

"Stop it!" Lyra yelled, the steering wheel slipping through her fingers as she turned her attention from the road to push at her mother again. "Sit down!"

"No!"

This time Paula's entire body came over the con-sole, pushing Lyra back against the seat. Her arms in-stinctively went up to ward off Paula's flailing limbs. She felt the car swerve and pushed her feet against the floor hoping she was hitting the break, but it was the gas. The vehicle took off, where Lyra had no idea be-cause she couldn't see anything past her mother's small head and screaming mouth.

"I'm sick of you, too!" Paula was screaming. "Let me out of here!"

Lyra finally grabbed both her mother's wrists and pushed her back just in time to hear the screeching of the car tires. Paula screamed and Lyra reached around her to grab the wheel, but her fingers slid off it again. There was more screaming and more swerving and Ly-ra's head rang with all the noise. Then there was a loud crash and the tears in Lyra's eyes seemed to freeze right there. Suddenly Paula wasn't on top of her any-more and the car wasn't swerving. She wanted to open her eyes but she couldn't. They felt wet, not just closed.

Her chest hurt and she felt like she should scream again, but couldn't.

It was dark. So very dark Lyra felt an edge of panic. Then she felt nothing.

Chapter 21

At the Big House Janean and Regan had gone into the kitchen to get coffee. Bruce, Savian, Adam, Trent and Sean sat in the living room. Dion paced, looking at his watch every few minutes and checking his cell phone just as frequently.

He'd called Lyra more than a dozen times but hadn't received an answer. To say he was worried was an understatement. But he couldn't go to her now. The family needed to discuss what had happened at the ball after Lyra left and how they were going to conduct damage control.

"They're both being booked for attempted murder and aggravated assault. Katrina's facing an added fraud charge for two Miami men that she swindled out of money. The ninety-year-old tycoon in L.A. and the businessman in Vegas will have to wait until she can be extradited to get their revenge," Trent filled them in. "Hopefully, she won't be out for a while."

"Does she have enough to make bail?" Savian asked from his spot on the couch.

Trent shook his head. "I checked her accounts a week ago, she's pretty low on funds."

"That explains why she was so desperate to hook Dion," Sean said.

Adam nodded in agreement. "And that's why she messed up. Greed was distorting her mind."

"And Stanford?" Bruce asked. "What was distorting his mind?"

"Jealousy," Dion added without a second thought. "He'd warned me to stay away from Lyra."

"And you didn't listen," Savian said with a dry chuckle.

"You know me better than that" was Dion's reply.

"They both should have known this family better." Bruce finished off his drink and put his glass on the end table with a loud clank. "I want these two buried beneath the jail and I want a formal statement made to the press tomorrow about the arrest made at the ball."

"And what about the other incident?" Savian asked. He'd removed his bow tie and unbuttoned the first few buttons on his shirt. All their jackets had been thrown on the backs of the chairs as they came into the house.

"I can't believe they pulled Paula Anderson into their sordid games," Sean spoke up, squeezing the bridge of his nose. "It's a good thing Lyra was there to hustle her out of there."

"Not good," Bruce chafed. "I wish that woman would just go somewhere and leave Lyra alone."

"I second that" was Savian's reply.

Adam, who had been quiet for the bulk of the conversation, stood, slipping his hands into his pockets. "But they tried to kill her. I don't really see how that was going to help either of them."

"With Paula out of the picture, Stanford would have Lyra to himself. There's only one other thing besides her work that Lyra cares about and that's her mother," Dion said.

"No, son. I don't think that's true," Bruce told Dion directly. "She cares about you. Stanford's known that for quite some time, so hooking up with Katrina would serve his purpose in getting you out of Lyra's life, as well."

"He's right," Trent said. "They were both banking on Paula's death to bring them what they wanted."

The room went quiet momentarily, then the loud crashing of glass hitting the hardwood floor brought them all to their feet. They rushed into the kitchen to find Janean holding the phone in one hand, her head falling back and a gut-wrenching scream escaping her throat. Regan was at her side.

"Aunt Janean, what did they say? What happened?" Regan was asking.

"Janean, what's wrong?" Bruce asked, going to stand beside his wife.

"She's dead," Janean said before falling to her knees and screaming even louder. "The car crashed and she's dead."

Her words echoed throughout the room and then there was a hushed whisper. "Who?" Dion asked with a lump already forming in his throat.

Janean looked up at him, tears streaming down her face. She never said the name, but she didn't have to.

Dion was out of the kitchen, pulling the front door open and storming out in seconds. Sean and Savian were right behind him.

"Wait, Dion! You don't even know where to go," Sean said, catching up to his brother and grabbing his arm.

"I'm going to her now, Sean! Don't try to stop me," he said, pulling out of his brother's grasp.

"Not going to stop you, man. Just hold up and let me drive."

Dion didn't argue but climbed into the passenger side of Sean's SUV, his heart pounding and tears stinging his eyes.

The drive to the hospital seemed to take forever. In the car, news of the accident was already hitting the airwaves. "One fatality is reported" was the only part of the announcement Dion kept replaying. Laying his head back on the headrest, he tried to keep his breathing steady, his nerves in check. It was one of the hardest things he'd ever had to do.

As soon as Sean pulled into the parking lot of the emergency room entrance, Dion leaped out of the vehicle and ran toward the doors. It was a Saturday night and more than a little chaotic with sick or injured people all around him and hospital staff trying their best to accommodate all of them. Dion grabbed the first nurse he saw by the arm.

"Lyra Anderson. Where is she?" he asked urgently.

The nurse, who was about half Dion's size with a cap of red hair and tired green eyes, looked up at him and mumbled, "Information desk's over that way, sir."

"Just tell me where she is?" Dion implored.

"You have to go to the information desk like everybody else," she replied, pulling her arm away from his grasp.

Cursing, Dion pushed past more people who seemed to be lost and flattened his palms on the counter of the so-called information desk. "Lyra Anderson?"

"And who are you?" the round Caucasian woman with fat, flushed cheeks and a messy graying ponytail answered glibly.

"I'm…" Dion hesitated.

"I'm her mother," he heard a voice from behind him say.

Janean stepped up behind her son, one hand going around his waist. "She was in a car accident," Janean continued, her voice still a little shaky, but much more composed than it had been when she was at the house.

The nurse began looking down at a clipboard filled with frayed edge papers. "Accident on Interstate 95's in exam room twelve. Fatality is on its way to the morgue. No names on either."

At that a quiet sob escaped Janean's lips.

"Thank you," Bruce said with an arm around his wife's shoulders as he escorted her away from the desk.

The three of them were headed into the massive waiting area when Trent and Savian came through what looked like two swinging side doors.

"Two of the cops on the scene are right down this way," Trent told them. "He's going to let us see them."

"See who?" Bruce asked.

Trent shrugged, his features stoic. "Both."

"I want to see Lyra" was Dion's reply.

This time Trent nodded and led the way. They all followed him through the same swinging doors he'd just emerged from. The next hallway was long, with doors on each side with signs numbering each exam room. In the center was a sort of island with computers and hospital staff moving around quickly. Orders were being shouted, machines beeped, codes were being called, and Dion ignored it all.

His gaze remained focused as he followed his cousins, his feet moving fast, his chest heaving with determination. Lyra wasn't dead. She couldn't be.

Exam room twelve was at the end of the next hallway, with two uniformed Miami police officers standing outside the room. They both looked pretty grim, one older cop holding a notepad and the younger one looking up just in time to see them coming.

"Reynolds, this is the Donovan family. Officers Troy Reynolds and Bobby Lynch," Trent said by way of introductions.

"Officers, what can you tell us?" Bruce asked, stepping forward immediately.

"I don't want to hear the story. I want to see Lyra," Dion said adamantly.

Sean touched his shoulders. "Let's just hear what they have to say first, then we'll go in."

Dion ran his hands down his face, taking deep breaths.

Reynolds, the young cop with the coffee-brown skin, began talking first. "Car swerved right after turning onto the interstate, jumped the jersey wall, went down the embankment and crashed. Fatality was ejected from the car upon impact. Body was found about twenty feet south of where the car landed."

"And the second person?" Savian asked, standing right behind his Aunt Janean with a hand in hers.

"Pretty banged up. She was wearing her seat belt, which along with the airbag most likely saved her life. The doctors seem to be optimistic, although I did hear them talking about surgery."

"Oh, Lord," Janean sobbed. "Where's Lyra Anderson?" she asked.

"We found this in the vehicle," Officer Lynch said, holding a small silver purse in his hand. "Identification belongs to Lyra Anderson."

"So where the hell is she?" Dion exploded. He'd heard enough. If he didn't see Lyra in the next few seconds he was going to hurt somebody.

Reynolds thrust a thumb toward the door behind him. Exam room twelve.

Without another thought Dion pushed past him, letting himself into the room, stopping cold the second he saw her lying in the bed.

Chapter 22

She lay absolutely still, her small body flanked by all the white of the sheets and the bandages. Beside her, machines with snakelike cords stretched to her arms, beeped and glowed with colorful numbers and lines. It smelled sterile, cold and still, like death.

Dion swallowed hard, still struggling to keep tears at bay. His chest heaved with the effort, his feet refusing to move even though his brain told him to go to her, touch her, save her.

After what seemed like a lifetime he took those first steps until he stopped right beside the bed, his hand reaching out to hers before pausing abruptly. Both her hands were bandaged all the way up to her elbows. He looked to her face and noticed dozens of small gashes across her cheeks, nose and forehead. They were red and slightly puffy. Her eyes were closed, her lips, too, as her chest moved rhythmically when she breathed.

Hours ago she'd been stunning in her pink gown and curly hair. Her face had been made up, lightly, but still so that she looked like a fairy princess. At least to Dion she did. All her hair was pulled back now, matted to her head beneath another swatch of bandages.

Behind him there was a noise, but Dion didn't turn. He couldn't take his eyes off Lyra.

"She has four broken ribs and multiple contusions. We'll know more about her neurological state when she wakes up. Right now the focus is on the extensive damage to her hands."

It was a male voice speaking and from what he was saying Dion suspected he was the doctor. Still not looking away he asked. "What's wrong with her hands?"

"I've ordered an orthopedic evaluation. The surgeon should be here soon. They were pretty banged up, like maybe she put her hands up to protect her face from all the flying glass. But then the air bag deployed and the force pushed her hands backward." The doctor lifted his hands to show Dion what he meant. "X-rays show broken bones in a couple of fingers and her right wrist. I won't know how much more damage occurred until she wakes up and the ortho examines her."

When Dion managed to look away from Lyra he saw that the doctor—a young African-American man with wire-rimmed glasses and a slightly receding hairline—was standing on the other side of Lyra's bed looking at him.

"She's very lucky. Mr. Donovan. Had she not been wearing a seat belt and that airbag not deployed, she would have gone straight through the windshield."

Dion nodded, swallowing hard. "Her mother?"

The doctor cleared his throat. "She died on impact. No suffering."

He nodded again, grateful for at least that. There was no love lost between him and Paula Anderson, but Lyra would want to know.

"Where's her body?"

"On its way to the hospital morgue," the doctor answered.

"Call me as soon as it's ready to be transported. I'll sign for an autopsy, as well." The decision was made before Dion had even spoken. He wanted to know what was in Paula's system when she died and if it was any type of poison he was determined Stanford and Katrina would stand trial for murder.

"Cause of death is most certainly going to be the ejection from the car. There's really no need for an autopsy."

Dion's cool look cut off the doctor's remaining words, so that he was the one nodding now. "I'll get the necessary paperwork to you."

"I want it expedited."

"No problem, Mr. Donovan."

"If there's nothing else, I'd like to be alone with her," he stated.

"Sure. I'll come back when the ortho arrives. See this red button here," he said to Dion, and waited for Dion to look where he was pointing.

"It's to call the nurse. If she opens her eyes, talks, shows any signs of waking up, call immediately. Do not hesitate."

"I will," Dion said solemnly.

The doctor left the room and Dion took another deep

breath. Looking down at her hands he sighed and closed his eyes. Saying a silent prayer, he gave thanks for her life and vowed to do whatever was necessary to make her future as happy as possible.

Time seemed to stand still while he sat by Lyra's bed, watching her breathe. He startled only slightly when he felt a hand on his back.

"Why don't you go home and get some rest," he heard his mother say.

"I want to be here when she wakes up."

"You'll probably be asleep, and how much good will that do?" Janean asked.

She'd changed her clothes, he noticed. This wasn't the same dress she'd worn when they'd come to the hospital with him originally. "What time is it?"

"It's almost noon. We've all been home, rested and come back. Now I want you to do the same."

"I'm not tired."

"Now you know better than to lie to me, Dion." Janean had her hands on his shoulders and leaned over to hug and kiss him on the cheek. "I know how you're feeling."

"No. You don't," he said, holding his head down. He'd always loved the comfort his mother provided, always knew he could turn to her whenever he needed to. Only now, it didn't seem like there was anything she could do to make this situation better.

"You think I haven't known all these years how you felt about this girl? I watched the two of you dancing around each other for years."

"And it didn't bother you?"

"No. Why would it bother me?"

"The rest of the family thinks I'm no good for her."

"Dion Lawrence Donovan, didn't I just tell you about lying to me?" she scolded.

Dion turned so he could look at her. "I'm not lying. They all think I'm just using her. They think I use all women. It's a well-known fact. I don't know how it skipped you." He stood and stretched then walked across the room.

"It must have skipped me and knocked you right upside your head," Janean said with a sigh. "Your family loves you. We respect you and are proud of the man you've become."

"Even if that man's always in the tabloids for womanizing?"

Janean chuckled. "Now you know there isn't a Donovan on this earth that can keep their name out of the mouths of jealous people. It comes with the name. That's why your father told me when I met him."

"But Dad didn't date a lot of women."

"That's what you think. He did his dipping and dabbling before he and I settled down. It's not against the law, Dion. And to tell the truth, I've never seen you disrespect a female. If you didn't want to be bothered with them anymore you told them so and moved on. There's nothing wrong with knowing what you want."

He turned, rested his hands on the foot of the hospital bed and looked at Lyra. "I've always wanted her."

"I know. And she's always wanted you. The good Lord spared her life because He wasn't finished with her yet. She'll be here for you to do right by her."

He nodded. "I will. She's had a hard life. Finding out about Paula isn't going to be easy."

Janean glanced down at Lyra and shook her head.

"No, it hasn't been easy. But you know, she's always been a fighter. No matter what kids used to say about her or her mother, she got up and went back to school the next day with only positive thoughts. She's the best thing to come from Paula Anderson."

"The very best thing," Dion said, silently urging Lyra to open her eyes and look at him.

When she didn't, Janean stood and walked to him. "Go on home, take a hot shower and eat something. I'll call you if anything changes."

He nodded because he knew she was right. As much as he didn't want to leave Lyra's side, there wasn't much he could do for her if he collapsed from fatigue himself. So with slow steps he moved to the side of her bed again, this time lowering himself to whisper in her ear.

"I'll be right back," he said, then kissed her cheek. "I love you."

When he stood and moved again, Janean opened her arms to him. He looked at the woman before him and could only smile. Never in Dion's life had he thought he could love another female as much as he loved Janean Donovan. Now he did, and his mother understood perfectly.

Chapter 23

Everything hurt. There was a wicked pain searing across her forehead and pressure on her shoulders. Her stomach churned, and when she attempted to lick her dry lips her cheeks throbbed. What the hell? Lyra thought, but then considered it might help to at least open her eyes.

She'd had hangovers before, mostly in college after finals. This didn't feel like a hangover. Actually, there was a haziness hovering around her, and opening her eyes felt like a tremendous chore. She'd only had two glasses of champagne at the ball, definitely not enough to cause a hangover. Still, her stomach felt as if it would momentarily heave whatever was inside and her temples felt like someone was driving nails into her head.

Lyra whimpered, the act of trying to open her eyes more tiring than she'd ever imagined.

"Lyra." She heard her name being called and wanted to open her eyes even more urgently. But she couldn't.

"Just relax, take it slow," the voice said. It was a man, a familiar man, she thought.

Lyra took a deep breath, let her eyes rest a minute, then attempted to open them again. This time it worked, her lids cracked open. Spears of light seeped inside and she whimpered again.

"I'll get them. Just sit tight. I'll take care of it," the male voice told her. She'd heard this voice before, felt soothed by it at one time.

When she tried to open her eyes this time they opened wider, the light subsided and she blinked long, then opened her eyes again. She saw Dion standing next to her and wanted to smile. But something like dread settled in her chest and she gasped instead.

"The car," she whispered, her throat a little sore with the effort.

Dion's lips closed into a tight line before he nodded. "There was an accident," he told her.

Flashes of memory sped through Lyra's mind and she gasped at the recall. The bright lights and fancy dresses at the ball, followed by the stench of alcohol, the slurred speech of her mother, the car moving fast, spinning out of control. With an audible cry she felt the impact of the crash once more and tears streamed down her face.

"It's all right, baby. Everything's all right now. You're at the hospital and they're taking good care of you," Dion attempted to reassure her, his hands wiping away the tears on her cheeks.

"She wouldn't put her seat belt on," she heard herself saying in a crackled voice. "I told her to put her seat belt on."

"Okay," Dion was saying.

But Lyra heard something else, beeping and doors opening and footsteps. She looked around and in the next instant there was a woman standing beside her.

"Ms. Anderson? Can you hear me?" the woman was saying.

Of course she could hear her, she wasn't deaf. "Yes," Lyra said, wanting the woman to go away.

She didn't, and in came another stranger. Lyra looked to Dion, who stared at her with concern. She closed her eyes and tried again to remember everything that had happened. He said there was an accident and she was obviously in the hospital. Okay, so that meant she was hurt. But she wasn't the only one in the car.

"My mother?" she asked, looking at Dion again. "Where's my mother?"

"I'd like to do a few tests, Mr. Donovan. If you could just step out of the room for a few minutes."

He was the doctor, Lyra supposed as she looked from him to Dion and asked again, "Where's my mother?"

Dion looked tired but he kept his eyes on hers after nodding to the doctor. "She didn't make it, baby" was what he said before leaning over to kiss her on the forehead.

Lyra's eyes closed again and this time she didn't really care if she could open them again or not. She didn't hear Dion leave the room and barely heard the doctor and nurse talking to her. All she heard was the screeching of the tires and the loud sickening crunch of metal that signaled the end.

Six days later, Lyra stood in the Canyon Pines Cemetery, a navy blue coffin draped with blue and white carnations only six feet away from her. Her tears had long since dried up. She'd cried for Paula Anderson for years, now all she could do was stand.

Janean and Bruce stood by her side as they had these past few days. When she'd been discharged from the hospital she'd returned to the Big House and to the bedroom where she'd grown up. Her hands were still bandaged and the date for her surgery was scheduled for next week. The impact of the air bag had caused severe nerve damage to both her hands. If not repaired, Lyra might not do something as simple as write her name again. And she might never hold a camera again. That thought made her extremely sad but not sad enough to cry. Lyra was definitely all cried out.

It was a bright sunny day in Miami, the day she had to bury her mother. The funeral service had been a wonderful heartfelt homegoing filled with friends of Paula's—friends Lyra never knew she had. Of course there had to be others in Paula's life, others that were trapped in the same addiction as her mother had been. Lyra silently prayed for them all, instead of judging them, because it's what her mother would have wanted.

Several of the Donovans were at the funeral. Regan and her parents, Savian and Parker. Sean was there and, of course, Dion, whom she hadn't spent a moment alone with since that day in the hospital when he'd told her that Paula was gone. It wasn't because Dion hadn't tried to see her alone, it was that Lyra didn't want to see him. Over the course of the past few days she'd had time to really think about what had happened and about all that had led her to this moment in her life.

The revelation that Mark was an idiot and her sleeping with Dion had been things she'd known were bound to happen. And really, Lyra didn't regret any of that. What did linger in her mind was Katrina's announcement that she was carrying Dion's child. She wondered if Dion knew, if he did and just wasn't telling her, or any of his family for that matter. She also wondered if his family knew and had agreed to keep it from her. All this made Lyra wonder if she'd ever be able to trust Dion, or if what was between them could really be expected to last.

Now was not the time to consider all these things. It was time to say her final farewell to her mother. When the preacher said his last words and nodded toward Lyra, she took one slow step toward the casket, then stopped.

"You've done all that a good daughter can do," Janean said into her ear. "You can go now."

Lyra shook her head. No, she couldn't. With a deep breath she walked the rest of the way to the casket and picked two bright white roses from one of the arrangements sitting on the ground. With steady hands and a heart that actually felt lighter than it had in years, she lay the two stems on top of her mother's casket and said, "I love you, always."

Bruce wrapped his arms around her whispering in her ear, "She was so very proud of you, Lyra. You were everything to her."

Lyra nodded, knowing his words were true. She would move on with her life knowing that her mother had been very sick for a very long time and that even in that sickness her love for her child had never ceased.

Lyra heard his voice, felt the comfort it exuded. Then she heard something else. A female's voice saying something she never wanted to hear—someone else would have Dion's child.

They'd all walked away from the burial site and were just about to step into the four limousines that were waiting for the family. Someone yelled, everybody stopped walking and looked around. Then shots rang out.

Lyra didn't have a chance to see where they came from as she was pushed immediately into the backseat of one of the limos. There were screams and yells all around as her heart thumped wildly in her chest.

"Dion," she whispered.

Chapter 24

Trent Donovan was still in Miami wrapping up his investigation of Katrina Saldana and uncovering even more disturbing facts about the woman and her connections. The fact that Katrina and Mark Stanford had made bail and were released from jail the day before Paula Anderson's funeral had concerned him.

"What should we do?" Sean asked Trent as he, Dion and Parker sat in Trent's hotel room.

"We should be alert" was Trent's response. "Stanford has a good lawyer and so does Katrina. Of the two of them I think Stanford's the most stable. He's not about to risk his job or his money over any more scandal. Katrina, on the other hand, doesn't have much to lose."

"What about the men pressing charges against her?" Parker asked. "Who are they and how far will they go to see her punished?"

"Most of them are old rich men who just want to punish her for making fools of them. One, however, is connected to some unsavory characters so it might be a little dangerous to her to be out of jail right now," Trent told them.

"So it would make sense for her to keep a low profile," Sean said.

Dion shook his head. "No. She won't do that. I'll see her again," he said with confidence. "I get the feeling she's not finished yet."

This conversation had led the Donovan men to hire security for the funeral, and it was a good thing they did.

Dion watched Lyra from a distance, his heart going out to her for all the pain and loss she had endured in her young lifetime. He wanted so badly to stand by her, to be the one to comfort her, but she didn't appear to want that. In the past few days she'd been very standoffish with him, so much so that he wondered where their relationship now stood.

It was selfish of him to stand here at this gravesite thinking about his future with a woman who was barely speaking to him. But Dion didn't care. He wanted Lyra, he wanted a life with her and he wouldn't apologize for thinking of nothing else.

When she faltered only slightly at the coffin he wanted to run to her side, to scoop her up into his arms and hold her away from any harm and pain forevermore. But his parents were there, that would have to suffice.

As they filed away heading to the limos, Dion couldn't help but look around. The funeral hadn't been private. Lyra had wanted all of Paula's friends to come and say their final farewells. So there were at least one hundred and fifty people around, some going to cars, others standing in groups lighting cigarettes or shaking their heads in either sorrow or disbelief.

He saw the bodyguards that they'd hired to stick close to the family for a couple of weeks as they seemed to be looking around just as he was. Then he saw Katrina.

Dion instantly moved away from the family, heading straight toward her. She was standing on the other side of the pebbled driveway, her hair pulled back into a ponytail, a short coat belted at her waist. Her legs were covered in some type of skintight denim, and stiletto heels adorned her feet. She was staring intently, Dion noted. But not at him.

He walked faster, trying not to draw attention to himself but needing to get to Katrina as soon as possible. When he was just at the front of one of the limousines Dion had to stop to let a car pass. Since there would be no official funeral procession this time, cars were free to go without waiting for the hearse or the family cars to pull out first. In the second he stood still he saw Katrina reach into her pocket and pull out a gun. Without wasting another second Dion ran toward Katrina, shouting for her to put the gun down.

She never wavered, didn't even look in his direction, but pulled the trigger.

Shots rang out as bullets pierced the windows of the limousine that Lyra was getting into.

All hell broke loose as Dion ran straight into Katrina knocking her to the ground. Two of the bodyguards were there in seconds, grabbing Katrina's arms and wrestling the gun out of her hands. When Dion rolled off her she was pushed onto her stomach and one of the guards held her hands behind her back.

"You don't love her!" she screamed at Dion. "You can't love her! She's nothing! Nobody!"

Dion looked down at what he once thought was a beautiful woman and shook his head. "She's more than you will ever be."

"Dion!"

Hearing his name being yelled pulled Dion's attention away from the pitiful sight of Katrina being lifted off the ground and held tightly by the bodyguards.

Lyra struggled to get away from another bodyguard who was trying to keep her in the limo, away from the commotion on this side of the driveway. He ran to her, giving the guard a nod of permission to let her go. When he thought Lyra would run into his arms she pushed past him to look over to where Katrina was being led away.

"You can't hurt her," she was saying, out of breath. "She's carrying your baby."

"What?" Dion asked pulling Lyra's arm and turning her to face him.

She brushed wayward strands of hair away from her face and took a deep breath. "At the ball she told me she was pregnant with your child."

"What the hell did she just say?" Bruce came up behind Lyra looking at Dion with a deep frown.

"Please God, say it's not true," Janean implored.

"Hold on. Wait just one damned minute," Dion roared. "Who told you this, Lyra?"

Folding her arms over her chest and looking him straight in the eye Lyra said, "Katrina said she was carrying your child."

For a few seconds that Dion figured everyone else

held their breath, he could only clench his teeth as anger seared through him. Looking over his shoulder he watched as the guards shoved Katrina into the back of one of the SUVs they drove. Turning back to Lyra and his family he stated slowly and precisely so that there would be no mistaking of what he had to say. "I did not impregnate that woman. She's a vengeful liar and an opportunist."

Janean gave an audible sigh of relief. But Lyra didn't look too impressed by his words.

"Lyra, baby, you know me," he said, and took a step toward her.

She was shaking her head. "I can't do this. It's too much," she said, tears filling her eyes. "All of it is just too much."

Dion reached for her but she stepped away. "I've never lied to you, Lyra. Ever. You know who I am and what I'm capable of."

"Leave me alone, Dion. For now, please, just leave me alone," she said slowly before walking away with Bruce heading after her.

When Dion made a move to follow her, Janean stepped up putting a hand to his chest. "Give her some time, son. She's just lost her mother."

"And I'm losing her," he said with pain racking his chest at the thought. "She doesn't believe me. She doesn't want me near her. I'm going to lose her."

"You're going to lose her if you push her. Not only does she have to deal with her mother's death, but Dion, she might not ever take another picture in her life. She's having surgery next week and her career future is unknown. And today of all days that lunatic woman was actually shooting at her. You've got to give her a moment to breathe or you will lose her, forever."

Taking a deep breath Dion listened to his mother's words, tried valiantly to absorb and accept them. "I love her so much."

"Then be the friend you've always been to her," Janean said seriously, patting a palm to her son's cheek. "Be there for her the way you used to be. Sometimes you have to go back to the basics."

With those parting words his mother was escorted into the same limo as Lyra. Dion stood in the grass watching as they pulled off, wondering if he could really go back to what he and Lyra used to be.

Chapter 25

The room was dim as Lyra lay on her back staring up at the ceiling. It had been eight weeks since the accident and two days after her third hand surgery. This one, Dr. Elias, the hand specialist, had told her, would be the last. If his attempts to save the nerves in both her hands didn't work this time, her condition would be permanent.

Lyra could feel her hands and she could move her fingers, but gripping or having any type of strength to do things such as hold a pencil or lift a fork to her mouth were touch and go. After each surgery she'd undergone intensive physical therapy that helped, but didn't prove one-hundred-percent effective. So tonight she lay here thinking of what her life would be like if full recovery was not an option.

After all she'd been through, Lyra refused to think

anything other than optimistically. She was still among the living, which meant she still had living to do. If she had to do something other than photography as a career, she would. And she would work as hard as she could to maintain her independence, because living with the Donovans for the rest of her adulthood was not an option. These days she loved this family even more than she had in the past and appreciated everything they did for her. She didn't feel like she owed them anything anymore, besides living her life to the fullest. As such she knew she had to leave this house and make a home of her own, on her own terms.

In thinking along those lines it was obvious that Dion would enter the picture. Although in the past weeks they hadn't been intimate, hadn't even talked about their relationship, Lyra couldn't deny that she still loved him and probably always would. Even before Dion's announcement that Katrina was definitely not pregnant based on a pregnancy test given to her in jail, Lyra had come to terms with Katrina's lies and vindictive actions. Additionally, she'd dismissed Mark's bitter betrayal. And she was profoundly thankful that the autopsy Dion ordered on her mother had not come back showing traces of any drug poisoning. It was all in the past now, and Lyra was determined to focus on her future.

When there was a light knock at her bedroom door she whispered, "Come in," thinking that it would be either Ms. Janean or Regan bringing her dinner, since she was still taking two painkillers that made walking up and down the stairs a treacherous task.

Her heart did a little flip when she looked up to see Dion carrying the tray of food and closing the door behind him.

The lamp on the side of her bed was on but it wasn't bright, and her blinds had been closed. For some reason bright light was giving her headaches. One of the doctors mentioned it might be post-traumatic stress after the accident. She just hoped it would be temporary. Watching Dion walk toward her, Lyra tried to sit up on the bed. He hurriedly put the tray on her nightstand and came closer to the bed to help her.

"Let me get the pillows for you," he said, and leaned over, adjusting pillows behind her head.

She couldn't help it, she inhaled, and the scent of his cologne sifted through her nostrils. She'd missed his scent so close to her.

"Thanks," she murmured, then tried to pull at the sheets to bring them up higher on her chest. They slipped out of her right hand and she had to use the left to pull the other side up.

"Mom said it's time for you to eat before you can take any more of your happy pills," he said jokingly as he moved to retrieve the tray again.

He wore jeans and a T-shirt and looked perfectly at home putting a tray of food in front of her while she sat up in bed. Funny how he could look just as good this way as he did all decked out in a tuxedo at a ball or in a boardroom donning a suit.

"They don't make me happy," she said, trying for a smile.

Dion laughed. "Sure they do, and they take away the pain."

"True," she admitted, even though she tried to be extra careful about not depending on the pills. The last thing she wanted was to become addicted to any type of pills, or anything for that matter.

"Therapy starts again tomorrow," he said, unfolding the napkin and placing it in her lap. He took the top off the plate and grinned. "Your favorite, sloppy joes and french fries."

Lyra smiled at the food. It was her favorite. "Did Ms. Janean cook this?"

"No. I did."

She looked at him skeptically. "You can't cook."

"I'm offended," he said, sitting on the edge of the bed removing the plastic wrap from the little container that held the ketchup for her French fries. "I live alone. I had to learn how to cook."

"I'm not convinced," she said, watching as he picked up a fry and dipped the tip into the ketchup. She'd never liked her ketchup over her French fries, always preferred to dip them so she could control how much was on each fry.

Dion extended the food to her mouth and waited.

"Come on, try it. How hard is it to drop some fries in grease and wait for them to brown?"

Raising a brow at him she accepted the fry and chewed. It wasn't bad. But the sandwich would be the test.

"Okay, you win, fries aren't difficult. But nobody makes sloppy joes like Ms. Janean."

"You're going to eat those words," he said, lifting half of the sandwich to her lips and waiting while she took a bite.

Lyra chewed and tasted, relished and smiled. "It's passable," she said, motioning for him to give her another bite.

"Aww, you just don't want to give me my due. I know it's good because I tasted it before I brought it to you."

"Afraid I was going to throw you and your nasty food out, I bet," she said after chewing. Lyra reached for her glass. Her fingers weren't bandaged, only her wrists, since that's where the incisions had been made. She could feel the cold condensation from the ice and the juice and took a moment to wrap her fingers around the glass securely before attempting to pick it up. With a little concentration she picked the glass up, watched as it lifted slowly. When the ice cubes began to rattle Dion covered her fingers with his and helped her move the glass the rest of the way to her lips.

"Take your time, baby. I'm right here to help you," he said, his gaze steady on hers.

She leaned forward a little to touch her lips to the glass and take a sip. After swallowing, she let Dion guide the glass back down to the tray. "Thanks."

"It'll be okay," he said, keeping his fingers on hers. "Like I said, therapy starts again tomorrow and everyone's really optimistic about the surgery this time."

Lyra nodded. "I know. It's just going to take some time."

"Right. So for the moment I'll be at your beck and call doing whatever you need me to do."

"Ms. Janean and Regan have been here."

"I know, but I told them I wanted to help. Is that a problem?"

She shook her head. "The magazine's doing really well. I know you have work to do."

"And I'll be sure to do my work, but when I can I want to be with you. Will you let me do that, Lyra?"

She waited a beat, wondering if there was a reason why she shouldn't take help from her best friend. When no reason came, she smiled. "Only if I can finish eating my dinner."

Dion's response was quick laughter that warmed Lyra all over. "Your wish is my command," he said, lifting the sandwich to her mouth again.

"So the show for Camille is in development. Regan's working on her first live fashion segment that will follow the early-evening news broadcast," Sean reported at their monthly meeting.

"Good. Good," Reginald said. "We're moving in the right direction."

"I'm hearing a lot of buzz around the relationship advice column, too," Dion added. "Is that something we might want to expand on?"

Sean tapped his pen on his notepad. "I was thinking about that, but I want to read a few more posts first. We had a new 'Jenny' start about six months ago. Since then the letters asking for advice have increased. I just want to make sure we're producing steady numbers for a while longer before we think of expanding."

"Right now it's just a quarter page column. She's answering, what, two letters a magazine?" Dion asked.

"Correct" was Sean's reply.

"If the numbers are growing, the least we can do is expand to a full page, with replies to four to six letters per magazine. See how it does after that," Bruce suggested.

Dion nodded. "I agree."

Sean still looked a little skeptical. Actually, he looked doubtful or worried, Dion couldn't put his finger on which. In the past weeks he'd been so caught up in what was going on with Lyra and her recovery he hadn't had much time to talk to Sean about anything but business. He made a mental note to do that, because something was definitely bothering his younger brother.

"Let me talk to the writer first, see where her head is regarding expansion. Can we address this again at next month's meeting?" he asked, looking directly at Dion.

Supporting his brother's decision and respecting the fact that Sean was the expert on the magazine's distribution and expansion efforts, Dion nodded. "Sure. We'll put it on next month's agenda."

"Any word on when Lyra will be back to work?" Savian asked, bringing utter silence to the room.

Everyone looked to Dion for an answer, but Regan spoke first. "I think she needs a little more time. Therapy's been good, but I don't know how confident she is right now."

"She's getting better," Dion offered. "But I think Regan's right, we should give her more time."

Bruce nodded. "I agree. Let the other staff photographers handle things for now."

"We want her in tip-top shape when Fashion Week kicks off, so giving her a rest now is a good idea," Regan added.

Dion wanted her in tip-top shape regardless of Fashion Week or any other business venture. That light of excitement whenever Lyra picked up a camera or snapped what she thought was the perfect shot had been absent from her eyes since the accident. That's what he wanted back, first and foremost.

Chapter 26

It had been raining all day. Lyra had grown tired of hearing the steady pat of water against the windows in her bedroom. She'd showered and dressed in jeans and an oversize sweatshirt. It was Sunday afternoon, so the Donovans would be at church, or so she hoped.

Over the past few weeks she'd rarely had more than a few moments alone, and the moments she was alone she usually fell asleep. But today she hadn't needed any pain medication and felt more energized then she had in a very long time. She wanted to walk outside to feel the breeze against her skin and to breathe, just to breathe.

On impulse she grabbed her camera and headed out the back door. It was quiet, as the rain had slowed to a dewy drip. The palm trees draped heavily and the close-cut grass glistened with moisture. She walked past the pool first, taking her time on the slick tiles as she passed. A breeze blew and the water in the pool rippled lightly. Instinctively Lyra stopped walking and lifted the camera in her hands. The fingers on her left hand shook a little as she grasped the camera, putting it up to her eye. Her right hand stayed steady as she positioned her finger over the shutter release.

A moment slipped by and the breeze blew again. Lyra watched the ripples, felt the beat of her heart pick up minutely, then pressed the release. It was a slow action, her finger moving just a few seconds after she decided to take the shot. But it had acted, she had controlled her fingers over the camera and with the tell-tale click of the camera that she'd missed immeasurably, a picture was taken.

With a smile on her lips Lyra headed for the dock, moving over the rain-slicked wood with measured steps. When she was close to the end she lifted her camera again and snapped. The clouds still hung low and dark in the sky, as if they would fall right into the water at any moment. As for the water, it looked dark and ominous. Each shot she clicked off caught the sight.

A boat was on the horizon, moving slowly through the graying backdrop. She took its picture with her heart hammering wildly against her chest.

"Lyra." He called her name from behind.

She knew it was him and wanted to run to him and jump into his arms she was so happy. Instead she turned slowly, camera still in hand. And when he was in view she pressed her finger on the release once more. There was a click and a flash and he blinked momentarily before his lips began to spread into a smile.

"The perfect shot," she said, smiling back at Dion.

He walked to her and as he did she snapped one,

then two, then three more shots of him. When he was close enough he touched his fingers lightly to both her wrists. "You're taking pictures in the rain?"

Lyra came up on her tiptoes and kissed his lips. "I'm breathing," she said on a giggle. "After all this time I'm finally breathing."

His message said to meet him here and Lyra figured it was appropriate since she was starving. She'd been working half days at the magazine for a little over a week now, taking it very slow, mostly approving pictures and working on her own private shots.

Dion checked on her several times in the hours that she worked and made sure to escort her out of the building to the waiting car that would drive her back home. The doctors still hadn't released her to drive alone yet, as her hands could be unpredictable. But they were going to get better, Lyra was certain of it.

So here she was at Shorty's again, the place that seemed to be the spot for her and Dion. He hadn't arrived yet, so she found them a booth and ordered water and beers for the both of them. Her cell phone rang and she reached into her purse to grab it. The action went smoothly as she'd used her left hand versus her right and put the phone to her ear after clicking it on.

"Hello?"

"You are not going to believe this!" Regan yelled on the other end as soon as Lyra answered.

"What's up?"

"I'm going to kill him, that's what's up! He's an arrogant, snotty little brat who thinks the sun rises and sets on his root beer–toned skin. I'm so sick of him at this moment I feel like choking him!"

Lyra simply nodded, with no clue as to what Regan was talking about.

"I mean really, how difficult is it to schedule an interview? Just have your secretary return my call and plug a date on your calendar. I'm doing him a favor! I shouldn't have to beg to give him this free publicity!"

The rant continued until Lyra interrupted with, "Ah, Regan, who are you talking about?"

"Huh? What?" Regan asked.

"Who won't grant you an interview?"

"That damned Gavin Lucas! I cannot stand him. He's been a pain in the butt since kindergarten and now he's creating havoc with my business."

Lyra tried not to smile. Gavin Lucas was the owner of Spaga, the restaurant she and Regan had enjoyed lunch at months ago. He was an up-and-coming entrepreneur in the Miami area, and *Infinity* wanted to do a complete story on his rise from sous-chef to owner of his own specialty chain of restaurants spreading along the East Coast. The uncles had decided to put Regan in charge of the story. Lyra wondered now if it were some sort of punishment on their behalf.

"Honey, I really don't think he's being difficult on purpose. Of course he knows how big an opportunity this could be for him and his business," Lyra said optimistically.

Regan was not trying to hear it.

"He's an ass! Plain and simple. I've left five messages for him this week alone and have received no response. I'm not going to keep chasing him around."

"I agree, you shouldn't call him again. Maybe pay him a visit," Lyra suggested. "I mean you two know each other outside of the business arena. Just show up one day and ask for the interview. He won't be able to avoid you if you're in his face."

"You're right," Regan said after a few moments. "Absolutely right. But if he does try to ignore me I'm choking him!"

Lyra laughed. "No, you're not. You've got too much class for that."

"Nobody knows that but you," Regan said, laughing herself. "Where are you anyway?"

"Waiting for Dion at Shorty's."

"I don't know why the two of you love that place so much. Well, I'll let you get to your date. Thanks for the suggestion."

"No problem. And no choking anyone."

"Right." Regan laughed before disconnecting the line.

She was smiling when he approached the table, slipping her cell phone into her purse. In the days since Dion had first seen her taking pictures out in the rain he'd seen Lyra smiling a lot. He'd also seen that little spark in her eyes when she did. He liked both.

"Happy to see me?" he said sliding into the booth across from her.

"Yes, but that's not why I'm smiling. Regan is flipping out over the Gavin Lucas interview."

"Oh, that," he said with a grin of his own. "Those two have been butting heads since grade school. This interview should be interesting."

"I don't understand why they gave it to Regan. She usually does the fashion work."

"Uncle Reginald figured it was best, since she knows Lucas."

"But don't the rest of you know him, too?"

"Not like Regan."

"No, Regan hates him."

Dion chuckled. "We know."

Lyra finally caught on. "That's cruel."

"Regan will be fine, she just needs to learn how to rein in her temper. But I didn't invite you here to talk about Regan," he said, signaling for the waiter so they could order.

When the orders were in she looked at him expectantly. "Okay, so why did you invite me here?"

"Because I have a present for you," he said, reaching into the bag he'd brought with him.

Dion placed the box on the table and watched as her eyes went from the box to his face then back to the box again.

"It's not my birthday," she said.

"I'm aware of that."

She waved a hand at him. "I meant, why did you get me a present when we both know it's not my birthday?"

"Because I wanted to," he told her, pushing the box closer to her. "Now, before you open it I want to tell you something."

He knew she wanted to open it immediately. Her fingers probably tingled with anticipation the way they always seemed to do when she was faced with a gift. He remembered many Christmases when they'd all trudged down the steps to open gifts. He and Sean had always raced to open their boxes while Lyra had taken her time, carefully unwrapping each gift that had her name on it. Even though she'd moved slowly, removing the tape as neatly as she possibly could, then folding the wrapping papers as if somebody was actually going to save it, her eyes had given her anticipation away. Just as they did now.

"Okay, what do you want to tell me?" she asked, folding her arms on the table and leaning forward to watch him eagerly.

He almost laughed at her struggle for patience but instead he reached across the table, taking both of her hands in his. Slowly, his thumbs scraped over the short scars left at both her wrists from her surgery. He lifted each to his mouth and kissed.

"I thought I lost you in that accident," he began, his voice low, deeper than he'd anticipated. "Then afterward, when you were alive but you wouldn't talk to me, it still felt like I'd lost you."

"I apologize for pushing you away," she began to say, but Dion silenced her with a shake of his head.

"No need to apologize. I should have been more sympathetic to your needs. I can't believe how hard that was for me, considering how close we've been over the years."

"You've always been sympathetic to me, Dion."

"That's why it shouldn't have been so hard. But this time it was and it took me a while to figure out why. I mean, I've known this for quite some time now, but it really hit me when you were sick."

"What's that?"

"I love you, Lyra."

She smiled at him and replied, "I love you, too, Dion."

He shook his head because even though this was the first time they were both openly admitting this to each other, he didn't think Lyra was really hearing him.

"I've loved you for years. It's been a part of me like

eating and drinking. There hasn't been a day in years that I haven't thought about you, needed to see you or speak to you. And even though you were miles away there was never a moment that I thought I wouldn't be able to do either or both. As you've said on many occasions, I'm used to getting what I want, when I want."

"That's true," she said, clasping her fingers tighter in his. "But it's a fault I try to overlook."

Dion smiled. "Thank you for that. What I'm trying to tell you, Lyra, is that I've never loved another woman, except my mother and my family. Ever. You are the first and the only. You are everything to me because you know all my good and bad traits and, as you just stated, you overlook most of them. I love you more than my own life and I want to spend our future making you feel as special and cherished as you are." He removed his hands from hers, lifted the box and placed it in her hands.

She looked at the box, running her fingers over the pink satin bow. He could tell that she didn't anticipate what was actually in the box because it was too big. But she seemed excited just the same.

Dion waited while she untied the bow and sat it to the side. She peeled back the floral paper and folded it neatly. Just as he knew she would.

When she lifted the top and pushed past the tissue paper Dion held his breath.

Lyra gasped. "It's the picture I took of you on the dock the other day. Where did you get this?"

"I came into your studio when you were looking at them, remember? When you looked away I swiped one."

"And I drove myself crazy for the hour after that swearing I had another photo but couldn't find it."

"Sorry," he said with a chuckle. "There's something else."

Lyra looked into the box again, and tied with the same colored ribbon that had adorned the box was a diamond ring. She looked up at him, then down at the ring.

Dion picked it up and lifted her left hand. "Now you can wear my ring on your finger and have my picture on your desk."

When she didn't speak he lifted her hand to his lips, kissing the ring on her finger. "And you can have my heart forever if you want it."

Chapter 27

Two hours later Lyra still hadn't answered Dion's proposal. They were at his condo sitting on his couch after enjoying a glass of wine. She wondered if he was still waiting for the answer and smiled inwardly at the fact that he probably was.

"I want you to strip for me," she said when they'd sat in silence a few minutes.

"What?" he asked looking at her strangely.

"You heard me. Strip."

With a nod he stood and reached out for her hand. "Come on, let's go into the bedroom."

Lyra shook her head. "No. Right here. Right now, I want you to strip."

He gave her a smile, that intensely sexy one that sent sparks of lust darting throughout her body. When he stood, he pushed the two tables back and bent down to remove his shoes. Lyra lifted her glass of wine and took a sip as she sat back and watched him.

His fingers went to his belt buckle first as he unclasped it and pulled it free of the hoops. He flattened his hand over his already swelling erection and Lyra sipped her wine again.

"See something you like?" he asked.

Lyra licked her lips. "I don't see enough" was her reply.

With a nod and a devilish grin Dion pulled his shirt free of his pants and lifted it over his head. His chest was bare as he made his pectoral muscles jump on command. "Cute," she said with a sigh.

When his fingers went back to his pants he undid the button and slid the zipper down slowly. He turned around, gave her his back as he let the pants slip from his hips, then stepped completely out of them.

"More." She beckoned.

He obliged by slipping his fingers beneath the band of his boxers, pushing them over his hips, down his thighs and to the floor. His muscled buttocks still faced her and she looked him over with sexual hunger building steadily inside.

"Turn around," she said, her throat feeling a little dry even though she'd just had another sip of her wine.

Dion turned, wrapping his fingers around his length and stroking it in front of her. "See something you like now?"

"That depends," she said, scooting to the edge of the chair.

"On what?"

"On how good it goes with my wine."

Dipping her finger into her glass she touched the tip

of his erection, watching intently as a drop of the wine slid over his hardness. Dion moved his fingers just as she extended her tongue to lick the wine away. "Hmm," she said. "Goes well with a dessert wine."

Lavishing his length with her tongue over and over, Lyra was rewarded with Dion's groaning, his fingers delving deep into her hair, until he could bear the tortuous pleasure no more. He pulled her head away.

"Your turn," he said in a strained voice. "Strip."

Desire pooled in her stomach, reaching greedy hands toward her center where she was achingly wet and ready. So Lyra wasted no time standing and removing her own clothes until she stood naked in front of him.

He reached for her then, pulling her to him for a kiss that blazed every inch of her body but focused solely on her tongue. Wrapping her arms around his neck and pressing even closer to him, Lyra took the kiss and ached for more. Nobody had ever kissed her like Dion Donovan. Nobody had ever made her feel the way this man did. Lyra had never truly known the meaning of the word desire until he'd put his lips on her. Now, she knew she would desire this Donovan for the rest of her life.

It took momentous strength to pull away from that kiss, but Lyra did it. Then she placed her palms on his chest and licked over his taut nipples until he was whispering her name. When she pushed him back onto the couch he looked startled. She smiled as she straddled him, reaching a hand between them so she could guide his length into her opening.

"You asked me a question earlier," she said, slowly lowering herself onto his thickness.

His hands gripped her face as the rest of his body held perfectly still. "Want me to ask you again?"

Lyra nodded and eased down onto him another excruciatingly slow inch.

"Marry me, Lyra. Be my wife, my love, my heart and soul forever?"

On a gasp Lyra was completely impaled by him. Dion sucked in a breath. She leaned closer until her forehead rested on his. "Yes," she whispered, then began to ride. "Yes. Yes. Yes."

* * * * *

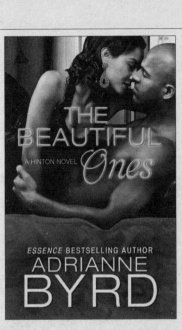

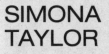

REQUEST YOUR FREE BOOKS!

2 FREE NOVELS
PLUS 2 FREE GIFTS!

KIMANI™ ROMANCE

Love's ultimate destination!

KROM11B

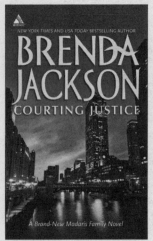